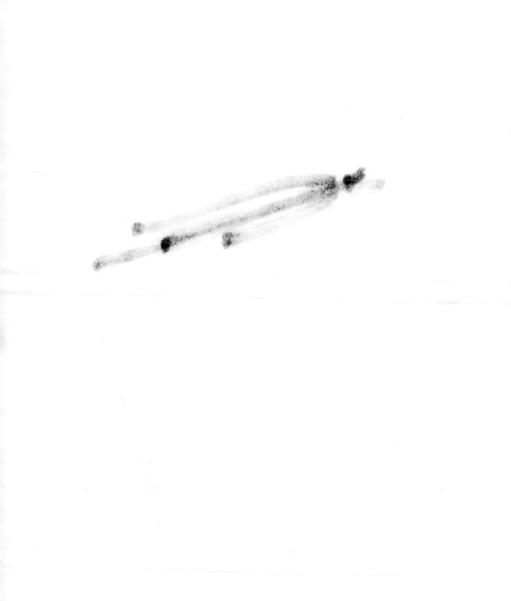

Icarus World Issues Series

On Heroes and the Heroic
In Search of Good Deeds

Series Editors, Roger Rosen and Patra McSharry Sevastiades

THE ROSEN PUBLISHING GROUP, INC.
NEW YORK

Published in 1993 by The Rosen Publishing Group, Inc.
29 E. 21st Street, New York, NY 10010

First Edition

Library of Congress Cataloging-in-Publication Data

On heroes and the heroic : in search of good deeds / series editors, Roger Rosen and Patra McSharry.
    p.   cm. — (Icarus world issue series)
    Includes bibliographical references and index.
    Summary: Presents a collection of essays examining the notion of the hero, the anti-hero, and heroic deeds in history and contemporary life.
    ISBN 0-8239-1384-8 (hc) -- ISBN 0-8239-1385-6 (pb)
    1. Heroes — Literary collections. 2. Courage — Literary collections. 3. Heroes — Juvenile literature. 4. Courage — Juvenile literature. [1. Heroes. 2. Courage.] I. Rosen, Roger. II. McSharry, Patra. III. Series.
PN6071.H406 1993
808.8'0352 — dc20   93-15167
                                                                          CIP
                                                                          AC

Manufactured in the United States of America

Contents

Introduction

Our moment in the world is one that finds us very uncomfortable with the notion of heroes. It simply doesn't square with the way our fiber has been molded and moved to accept the highest ideals of egalitarianism, the way we have embraced democracy as the greatest specimen of all the bodies politic trudging away on their Stairmasters. Those who sprinkle comparatives through their speech are downright suspect, for the universe of better and worse, taller and shorter, thinner and fatter is a place of judgment, and we tend to feel as though we stand accused. We quite naturally regard our accusers with a certain antipathy. Those with the boisterous confidence to employ superlatives, those ever so grand proclamations that proclaim the great great, can only be fools, madmen, or monsters: fools because who else could show such crude sensibility, throwing away all the qualifiers demanded by context that serve to render the thinking person mute; madmen to fly in the face of the carefully calibrated balance by which decent society steadies itself; monsters who are capable of moving beyond speech into action, plunging us into flames with the fire of their conviction. Simply put, we have, for the most part, lost our appreciation for martial music. Now when the posters get too large, and the face of our hero is seen everywhere, and his voice reaches us even in the shower, we know enough to know that we might be grappling with a "cult of personality." And those who have fought that fight can also take credit for sharpening the olfactory sense of plenty of stuffed noses, honing the talent to discern from a distance the early putrefying stench of tyranny.

In 1841, the Scottish essayist and historian Thomas Carlyle published a book entitled *On Heroes, Hero-Worship and the Heroic in History*, based on a series of lectures he had given between the years 1837 and 1840. His six categories of hero correspond to the six lectures he delivered: The Hero as Divinity, The Hero as Prophet, The Hero as Poet, The Hero as Priest, The Hero as Man of Letters, The Hero as King. Included in his examination are men such as Mohammed, Dante, Shakespeare, Luther, Burns, Rousseau, Cromwell, Napoleon. They are seen through this prism: "Worship of a Hero is transcendent admiration of a Great Man. I say great men are still admirable; I say there is, at bottom, nothing else admirable! No nobler feeling than this of admiration for one higher than himself dwells in the breast of man. It is to this hour, and at all hours, the vivifying influence in man's life."

This, along with other thoughts of Carlyle, formed a large portion of the belief system to which I was introduced as a teenager. A quirky education, you well might say, but I would venture to reply that many schooled in notions of various hierarchies toward excellence would have been so formed, whether or not they knew Carlyle to have been the source. "In all epochs of the world's history, we shall find the Great Man to have been the indispensable savior of his epoch;—the lightning, without which the fuel never would have burnt. The History of the World, I said already, was the Biography of Great Men."

What can we make of these nineteenth-century convictions one hundred fifty-three years after they were published? What is greatness in a society that makes little distinction between celebrity and notoriety? How does it transpire that someone can be a hero one day under one regime and a villain the next under another? Must greatness always affect great numbers? Who is worthy of our veneration? How do we know? Who sets these criteria anyway? The tenth volume of *Icarus*, "On Heroes and the Heroic: In Search of Good Deeds" sets out to explore these questions. As we take you to various places on the planet, reveal various forms, interpretations, and puzzles about heroism, we're certain you'll have even more questions than when you started. That's the way we want it.

Here, then, are nine new faces of the hero with one thousand—our contribution to the one never-ending story. And whether your meditations begin with John Wayne or Aleksandr Solzhenitsyn, whether you choose to wander with Marcel Kurpershoek's Bedouin Knight or Yeshayahu Koren's Israeli reservist, perhaps you will come to a place not dissimilar from my own, the place from whence you can hear the first call to adventure.

Roger Rosen, Editor

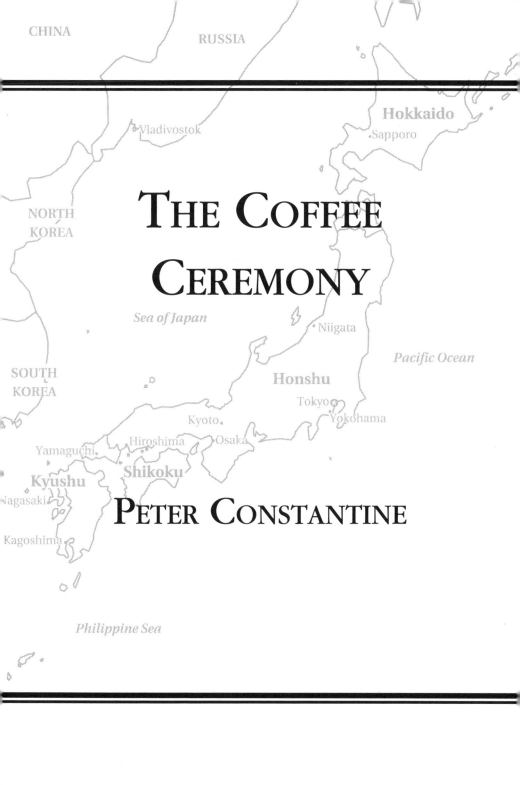

THE COFFEE CEREMONY

PETER CONSTANTINE

Peter Constantine was born in London in 1963 and spent his youth in Austria and Greece. He is fluent in six languages.

Mr. Constantine was trained in classical ballet in Europe and the United States and in 1981 made his debut in the international Theater an der Wien dance competition. From 1981 to 1987 he performed in dance companies throughout the world. At age twenty-four, he was injured and retired. For the next few years, he worked as an international representative for Hilton Hotels.

Mr. Constantine has been writing full time since 1990. He is the author of *Japanese Street Slang*. His forthcoming books *Japan's Sex Trade* and *Inside Japanese Slang* will be published by Charles Tuttle & Co. in fall 1993.

On a hot afternoon in May the white and pink cherry blossoms were still flowering in Seijo, one of the more affluent parts of Tokyo. Mrs. Ono was shuffling along the sidewalk in her *zoris* and her tomato-red kimono. She was a large and unathletic woman in her mid-fifties, but her eager round face and her childish dimples gave a strong impression of youthfulness.

"Oya-ma!" she snapped, wishing she had worn totes and the comfortable caftan her husband had brought back from his business trip to Europe. Breathing heavily, her fleshy knees beginning to sweat under the heavy silk, she reached into her handbag and, hiding her perfume bottle behind the large plastic-crocodile clasp and flicking her eyes left and right, she squirted the last of the fragrant liquid over her ample breasts.

"Hanaya Avenue, number 334!" She repeated to herself, carefully stepping around puddles and little mounds of what she referred to rather boldly as *inu no fun*, dog manure. She scowled at a woman who was hurriedly making a getaway with a neat frilly poodle on a leash. No lady of quality could be seen visiting someone's house, especially someone she had never met before, with less than immaculate sandals.

Mrs. Ono was looking forward to meeting Mrs. Suzuki. She had just joined the Tokyo Society Ladies Golf Club, of which Mrs. Suzuki was a founding member, and had been invited for coffee by phone with what she considered patronizing familiarity. Mrs. Suzuki had lost no opportunity to remind her that *her* husband was president of Happy Fondle Pet Foods International, which was about to merge with the financially strapped Poodle Perfume Inc., owned by Mrs. Ono's husband. Mrs. Ono had not been amused. On her very first day at the golf club, another member had launched into an endless account of Mrs. Suzuki's social prowess, rendering in breathtaking detail the maneuvers with which she had vanquished even her most ruthless rivals.

Mrs. Ono turned onto Hanaya Avenue, and seeing the stately minimansion number 334 with its small but expensive green garden, she broke into an eager trot, putting on a genial grin. In case she was being watched from the house, it was her duty, as a well-bred lady on a first coffee visit, to show brisk enthusiasm.

"Oh," her massive body proclaimed, "this is going to be such fun!"

Meanwhile, inside the house, Mrs. Suzuki moved back the heavy velvet curtains and cautiously peered out at the empty street. Craning forward, her nose touching the glass, she squinted eagerly past the row of boutiques, the post office, and the elegant villas that lined the asphalt all the way down to the station. Her eye caught a large spot in the distance moving eagerly toward her. She picked up her binoculars and trained them on the expansive kimono and the *zoris*.

"One and a half million yen!" she muttered, thoughtfully chewing her lip. "Late spring tomato-red—semiformal to formal, but much too bright for a woman that size—I've got a good five minutes to get ready."

She shoved the binoculars into the liquor cabinet and rushed to the anteroom where she had ready four kimonos of varying color and formality, a silk evening gown, a Spanish flamenco dress, and a pair of designer jeans carefully torn at the knee. With practiced fluency, she stepped out of her ankle-length French dress and slipped into a formal weed-green kimono that was sure to clash with the boisterous red that her approaching guest was wearing.

"We must outdo her," she said to herself, grimacing into the mirror, taken aback by the many fine wrinkles that she noticed under her eyes. She quickly dabbed white powder onto her face and neck to even out the Western look it had taken her forty minutes to achieve. Skidding over the parquet and snatching up a pair of embroidered guest slippers on the way, she raced into the kitchen, turned on the mocha-maker, and raced back out. In the hall she carefully laid out the slippers facing away from the door so that her guest, as custom dictates, could easily slip into them before entering the house.

The Suzuki residence was a sequence of spacious halls and rooms, some of them carefully Western with color-coordinated furniture, and some traditionally Japanese, sparsely laid out in beige and black with brown tatamis covering the wooden floors. Like her fashionable neighbors, Mrs. Suzuki kept three drawing rooms fully fortified and ready to entertain in. "A prepared hostess is a safe hostess!" was her motto. If, for instance, a guest were to materialize wearing a casual Chanel dress, she would be ushered into the trendy designer drawing room. If she were formally dressed (only yesterday Mrs. Miyazawa had almost taken her by surprise by appearing for a prenoon tea wearing a full-length taffeta evening gown), she would have been directed to the baroque dining room. If her guest had had the bad taste to appear in jeans or a jogging outfit (like Mrs. Inoue, the spring before last), she would be forced to accommodate her in the postmodern kitchen. Kimonos, however, whether informal or formal, demanded a traditional tatami-salon setting.

Sitting on the edge of the step that separated the hall from the living quarters, Mrs. Suzuki waited breathlessly for Mrs. Ono. She smiled as she delicately arranged the heavy green folds of her kimono around her feet.

There was a wooden clatter of sandals on the concrete garden path outside. Mrs. Suzuki jumped up. The sandals hesitated for exactly seven seconds as Mrs. Ono, mindful of etiquette, stopped to admire the artful Kamakura-period fish pond. Mrs. Suzuki put her ear to the door, wishing,

5

as she had on many previous occasions, that her husband had had the foresight to buy a more modern door with a peephole instead of this Edo-revival monstrosity.

"That man's fascination for antiques will be my undoing!" she hissed as she pressed her ear harder to the cold, polished copper panel that caught and amplified the sound of every movement and gesture guests made outside. She heard a diminutive plop as the handbag was set down on the gravel, followed by the rustle of silk. Mrs. Ono was obviously removing and folding her *haori*, the flimsy outer garment she wore as a jacket. Once the door was opened Mrs. Ono, as a lady of quality and a first-time guest, would be too busy bowing, greeting, and complimenting to struggle with her coat while clutching her handbag in one hand and balancing her present of expensive candied fruit in the other.

"Now comes the knock!" Mrs. Suzuki calculated with an eager smile. She slowly counted to ten, but nothing happened. She continued counting haltingly, breathing between counts, to fifteen, then twenty. There was still no knock. Mrs. Suzuki's lip trembled.

"She put that bag of hers down, four seconds—she slipped out of that ghastly tomato-tinted *haori*, ten seconds at most—she folded it, another five seconds! What in Buddha's name is the woman doing now, undressing?" Another forty-five seconds passed in silence.

Outside, Mrs. Ono was standing calm and serene on the first step of the patio. She sensed that she was being spied upon. She had decided to leave her hostess dangling and was gazing at the garden. There wasn't much to look at except for that frightful pond, but her face took on an expression of blissful rapture. Staring at a gray stone in the water, she counted to two hundred.

She heard a suspicious click from inside the house. Her blissful smile still intact, her eyes roved systematically over the facade. All the windows were closed and the velvet curtains drawn. Nothing moved. She ran her eyes suspiciously over the antique copper door: no peephole, not even a hidden one. There was no camera — she had checked the area over the portal and the cement base under and between the steps. She knew, however, that her actions were being monitored, and that the door, somehow or other, *had* to be the scanning post. Pretending to readjust the thong of her sandal, she sidled, hunched over, toward it.

In the hall Mrs. Suzuki, perplexed, ran through all the conceivable explanations for the strange scouring sound she was registering through the copper.

Outside, Mrs. Ono was crouching on one sandaled foot, swinging her other foot high in the air, careful not to touch the ground with it and smudge her immaculate white sock. To support her massive bulk (both her hands were busy working at the sandal), she leaned with her ear on the door. A passerby glancing into the garden would no doubt have seen only an unfortunate woman trying, with as much elegance as circumstances permitted, to fix her slipper. To keep her balance, she pressed her head harder to the copper to avoid toppling over. Inside, Mrs. Suzuki, bewildered at the uncanny sounds, settled with a rustle and a thump into a more favorable crouch.

Hearing the rustle and thump, Mrs. Ono bounded up to the balustrade to steady herself. The idea that she had caught her illustrious hostess, Mrs. Suzuki, wife of the perfidious president of Happy Fondle Pet Foods, on her knees, spying from her own hall, was almost more than her delicate constitution could take.

"I've got her, I've got her!" she croaked ecstatically.

She would have to move fast now. She checked her wristwatch; it was exactly four o'clock, the appointed coffee hour, which gave her fifteen minutes before she could be officially deemed late. She would now take a calm little walk in the garden. The disoriented Mrs. Suzuki would doubtless remain crouching by the door, as a lady of her distinction could not afford to be caught peeking out of a window. Mrs. Ono giggled discreetly to herself. She would put this advantageous situation to excellent use and set out to measure the garden by striding from one end to the other.

"It won't take long," she thought. "It's just a yard with a few shrubs and a puddle in it, after all, not a real garden."

This would also give her an opportunity to assess the size of her rival's villa and inspect its design and materials, for she had an uncanny gift for sizing up within a few yen the exact cost of any property she clapped her eyes on. She tiptoed off the patio and made her way to the far corner of the gate.

Disaster struck. It had rained the night before, and the earth around the perimeter of the garden was damp but firm — or so it seemed. No sooner had she taken three measured strides along the fence than her foot sank into a boggy patch of mud that was camouflaged by short thick grass. Mrs. Ono blanched. Not only was her *zori* caked with mud, but so was her immaculate sock. She panicked. "Water! A hose! An outside toilet! Anything!"

A cold sweat broke out on her powdered brow. Even if she could wash and dry her *zori*, which seemed unlikely, her sock would give her away even before she entered the house. In despair, she galloped toward the fish pond and, hitching up her kimono over her knees so she could squat down efficiently, quickly plunged the sandal into the water. Dodging the goldfish and toads, she rinsed it, praying fervently that Mrs. Suzuki would not emerge from the house on the pretext of picking a flower for a vase or watering something or other.

"Please, please, stay inside!" she begged, her full lips trembling. "I'll be ruined if that woman comes out now — I'll have to cancel my membership at the golf club!" Driven by despair, Mrs. Ono worked fast. She tore open her handbag and frantically raked through the lipsticks, powder puffs, folding fans, miniature sake cups, and spoons. She fished out the extra pair of white socks she carried in case of rain, but to her horror, she couldn't find the packet of tissues with which to dry the drenched sandal. Delirious, she snatched up the unfinished doily she was crocheting for the cocktail tray and hastily scrubbed and scoured her dripping, muddy sandal with it.

Repaired, freshly socked, and grateful at surviving this sudden blow of fate, Mrs. Ono humbly climbed the steps of the patio and knocked on the door. A religious woman, dedicated to both Buddhism and Shinto-animism, she firmly believed that the Buddha, if not the water spirit of the pond, had slapped her on the wrist for misbehaving, and she silently promised to mend her ways.

Hearing the shuffle of the approaching *zoris* for the second time, Mrs. Suzuki, furious at having been duped into crouching by the door for ten minutes, rushed off to the kitchen. It was her turn to leave Mrs. Ono in the lurch, although she knew she would have to open the door by the third knock.

"Hai!" she called out from the kitchen. "One moment, please!"

Mrs. Ono did not mind waiting. Mrs. Suzuki's slim formal figure finally appeared at the door. She looked at Mrs. Ono blankly, as if mistaking her for the perfume lady, or the free-lance hair stylist. "Yes?" she said curtly.

Mrs. Ono's beatific mood evaporated.

"I am Mrs. Ono, I have an appointment with your mistress!" she said with the perfunctory nod reserved for parlormaids.

Bubbling with fury but smiling pleasantly, Mrs. Suzuki became the perfect Japanese hostess.

"Oh, Mrs. Ono! Come in, come in! I am Mrs. Suzuki! How charming, how totally charming!" Each phrase she uttered in her melodious, high-pitched voice was accompanied by a

9

humble ninety-degree bow. Mrs. Ono too bowed repeatedly, uttering strings of apologies, compliments, and thanks.
She had quickly placed her jacket, handbag, and candied
fruit box in a neat pile by the door, which gave her hands
the freedom needed for elegant and socially correct bowing. Catching Mrs. Suzuki, who had not finished her incli-
nations, at a disadvantage, she quickly and with sardonic
deference pushed her present into the hostess's hands,
thus blocking her bow.

"It is only a small, boring thing!" Mrs. Ono purred in the
ancient formula.

"Oh, you shouldn't have bothered!" Mrs. Suzuki purred
back. Both women, filled with respectful loathing for each
other, smiled sweetly.

The two women eyed each other. Mrs. Ono's kimono, on
closer inspection, must have cost at least *two* and a half
million yen, and its fruity red color, Mrs. Suzuki realized
with rage, went uncommonly well with the large woman's
ruddy complexion. Her fingernails were too loud, and the
nail on her thumb was obviously a fake, but they were still
within the boundaries of propriety. "I wonder how she got
them to gloss that way?" Mrs. Suzuki pondered, her
friendly smile still intact, making a mental note to call her
beautician at the earliest opportunity.

Then the blood drained from her powdered face and she
felt sick to her stomach. Her eyes, still fresh and welcoming, stumbled over a horrendously large diamond on Mrs.
Ono's ring finger. How could she have missed it through
her binoculars? "That woman must have kept it hidden in
that perfidious handbag of hers and slipped it on at the
very last moment." The smile on Mrs. Suzuki's face almost
cracked. Mrs. Ono was quick to notice that Mrs. Suzuki
was hiding her bare ring finger, and surmised that soon it
would be covered with something quite exquisite.

All the while, Mrs. Ono was still bowing and murmuring charming words. As eye contact during bowing is frowned upon, Mrs. Ono, a master of etiquette, used this to her advantage. As her heavy torso moved forward and down, her eyes passed from the sparsely furnished hall to Mrs. Suzuki's irritatingly slim figure. On the way back up, she studied the intricate green designs of her rival's kimono. She was surprised at the formality of the frock. More suitable for a funeral than for afternoon coffee, she thought. She managed to convey her disapproval by staring at the garment with a look of mild, uncomprehending alarm. Mrs. Suzuki's smile became frostier as she elegantly indicated the slippers and the way to the tatami living room.

"What beautiful slippers, are they antique?" Mrs. Ono asked. She shuffled eagerly toward the hall step to take a closer look.

"Yes!" Mrs. Suzuki replied curtly, jolted by the hint that the house shoes she had laid out might be too dilapidated to offer a guest. "My husband's mother embroidered them," she said haughtily.

Mrs. Ono eyed them.

"The dear woman, how talented of her. All those little golden stitches! It must have taken her a whole year to do them all, how charming!"

Ignoring Mrs. Ono's venomous pleasantries, Mrs. Suzuki quickly positioned herself on the hall step leading to the inner rooms and peered at her uneasily. She felt that she had met this odious woman before, long ago, under very unpleasant circumstances that she could not quite remember. But ever the perfect hostess, she launched into a second round of traditional greetings.

"Please step up into the house," she said politely, pointing to the ancient slippers.

Mrs. Ono was always anxious about the ceremony of changing from street shoes to house shoes. She had to execute the whole ritual with delicacy and without using her hands: She would have to step out of her sandals and, in her socks, climb daintily up onto the step. There she would have to turn and, facing her hostess, step smoothly into the slippers, kneel down, and, balancing her heavy torso, humbly reposition her sandals from the center to the corner of the step. Then, while her hostess rushed to move the sandals back to the honorable center of the step, Mrs. Ono would be expected to heave herself up from her kneeling position in a single flowing motion and follow her hostess into the house. Mrs. Suzuki waited in anticipation.

Mrs. Ono drew in her breath and marched to the left side of the step. With the practiced elegance of a Kabuki actor, demurely bringing her delicate hand to her ample breasts, she stepped out of her sandals, a picture of maidenly grace. She modestly looked away from the slippers and, casting her eyes on the ground, climbed up onto the step. Then she made a quick half-step forward and decorously pressed her foot into the opening of the house shoe. Her smile froze and she tottered: The shoe was too small. Her large bunion was stuck. She realized that she would have to use her hand. That, however, was out of the question. She looked to her haughty hostess for help. Apparently oblivious to Mrs. Ono's plight, Mrs. Suzuki smiled and fluttered over to a vase to rearrange some flowers. Mrs. Ono thought of quickly using her hand to force her foot into the house shoe, but she resisted the temptation. If caught, she would be socially ruined.

"Oh, I am so sorry! The silly slipper! Too small, is it?" Mrs. Suzuki tittered. "I've never had this problem before! I am so devastated! Let me bring you my husband's new house shoes! No, I insist!"

Abandoning the flowers, she shuffled off, returning seconds later holding out a pair of ridiculously large slippers. There was now a prominent ruby on her ring finger.

Mrs. Ono, enraged at the humiliation visited upon her

feet, decided to lash out at the ring. She stared at it, ostentatiously confused at its sudden appearance; then, gazing at her own diamond for an unnaturally long time, she drew in her breath and did her best to look embarrassed. Mrs. Suzuki's lip trembled.

"Oh, is that a new ring? How charming!" Mrs. Ono trilled. "The red stone goes so well with your green kimono!"

The Zashiki drawing room, with its rich, sweet-smelling tatamis, was the sunniest and most serene room in the house. Mrs. Ono sat on a large cushion on the floor in the place of honor, with her back to an alcove cluttered with priceless vases and little statuettes. The shoji screens of translucent paper were half open, and the soft chime of a Korean wind harp tinkled outside in the breeze. Mrs. Suzuki had gone to the kitchen to prepare coffee. Mrs. Ono waited quietly. It would have been ill mannered of her to stare at the antiques, the flowers, or even the garden while her hostess was out of the room, so she cast her eyes down with gentle sensitivity.

In the kitchen, Mrs. Suzuki was pouring small amounts of the dark steaming liquid into every cup she could find, and was holding them, in turn, up to the light to check the translucency. She couldn't use heavy ceramic coffee cups—that would be too unrefined in a traditional tatami-room setting—but she couldn't rely on the fully translucent Japanese cups either; the dark liquid would jar the eye. She wiped small pearls of sweat from her upper lip. It was of critical importance with a woman like Mrs. Ono that she get the right lucidity. Her eye rested on a set of pale Nagasaki-Dutch cups that blended beautifully with her green kimono. After much deliberation, she decided they were Japanese enough for a traditional milieu, yet Western enough to set off the espresso-like coffee with charm. She poured two cups, and added, as she had learned from tea-ceremony rituals, a teaspoon of cold water to calm the hot liquid. She placed the silver coffee spoon on the far side of the saucer, with its stem facing to the right—she had established that Mrs. Ono was right-handed when her guest had offered the candied fruit at the door.

Satisfied that the coffee tray was in order, she shuffled back to the sitting room, brimming with tasteful apologies. Mrs. Ono saw the position of the spoon and, unable to resist the temptation, immediately became left-handed. She looked at the spoon with dismay, fumbled round the cup with her left hand, and brushing against the spoon knocked it off the saucer. The Korean wind harp tinkled loudly.

Looking up at her hostess's startled expression, Mrs. Ono froze. That face! It catapulted her back almost forty years. She was in her village in southern Kyushu, a dirty, squalid hamlet that she had disowned years ago. It was wartime, and the army had marched in and was rounding up teenage girls for the soldiers at the front in Southeast Asia.

She looked into her coffee cup and then at Mrs. Suzuki's pasty face.

She remembered the sea journey—the songs—the sea-sickness—the beautiful yellow cliffs of Korea—the wooden barracks in Burma—the pantaloons she had worn—the endless line of soldiers as she lay on her mat. She stared at Mrs. Suzuki and in her confusion declined one of the fruits she herself had brought.

In the garden the harp twanged and twanged.

They had been evacuated repeatedly as the front was pushed farther and farther back. "Work hard! Harder! The boys must be kept happy! Think of our nation!"

Mrs. Ono drank three cups of coffee and distractedly ate two pieces of candied fruit. She stared at the statues and the scrolls in the alcove and followed her frightened hostess around the garden. Bowing deeply, she thanked Mrs. Suzuki and in a daze hurried down Hanaya Avenue, past the expensive boutiques, past the post office and the station, until, turning off the main street, she disappeared from view.

THE MYTH OF
PAVLIK MOROZOV

YURI DRUZHNIKOV

Yuri Druzhnikov was born in Moscow in 1933. A historian, journalist, and writer, he is the author of several novels, research books, short story collections, and children's stories. He was a member of the Union of Soviet Writers until 1977, when he was blacklisted for publicly expressing his doubts about the veracity of Soviet propaganda concerning the boy-hero Pavlik Morozov. He was forbidden to publish and harassed by the KGB. Ten years later, he was finally given permission to emigrate from the Soviet Union.

Dr. Druzhnikov currently teaches Russian literature at the University of California, Davis. His most recent publications (in Russian) include *Angels on the Head of a Pin*; *Micronovels*; and *Prisoner of Russia: Understanding the Other Pushkin*. His articles have appeared in the *Washington Post*, the *New York Times, Novoe Russkoe Slovo*, and *Russkaya Mysl'*. He is an honorable member of International PEN.

In the period 1982–1984, Dr. Druzhnikov wrote *Voznesenie Pavlika Morozova* (The Myth of Pavlik Morozov). It was published in Russian in London in 1988. It has since been translated and published in Poland, Hungary, and Latvia, and will soon be released in Russia. The following selection was adapted from that work by Sonia Melnikova-Lavigne.

W̲hen I was eight years old, I sang in a children's choir. The conductor would announce proudly, "And now, with lyrics by the famous children's poet Sergei Mikhalkov and music by Hungarian Communist Ferentz Sabo—a song about Pavlik Morozov!"

Ours were not the only voices to be lifted in honor of the heroic Pavlik Morozov. For half a century, the whole country lauded this brave teenage boy. I need only recall some of the rhymes of Mikhalkov's song to give you an idea of Morozov's extraordinary reputation: Pavel/marvel, Revolution/execution, expose/depose, brave/grave, story/gory.

What was the deed that made him a hero? In 1932 Pavlik Morozov exposed his father as an "enemy of the people." He informed the OGPU (as the KGB, or Soviet secret police, was then called) that his father was helping the kulaks, successful peasants who refused to relinquish their land and livestock to the State for the Collectivization Plan*, and was therefore an enemy of socialism. Pavlik's father was arrested, tried, and sent to a concentration camp, never to be seen again. Soon after his father's trial, Pavlik was murdered by "enemies of the State." After his death, he was hailed as a hero of the people, and every child in the Soviet Union was required to learn his story and be prepared to follow his example.

---

*Collectivization Plan—a program of agricultural collectivization created by the Bolsheviks whereby agricultural land was forcibly nationalized, agricultural production was reorganized under state supervision, and produce requisitioned by the state. At the time, 80 percent of the population was peasants, who wanted to control the land they tilled. As a result, collectivization was resisted violently by many. The state responded with brutality, frequently executing those who resisted or exiling entire families to Siberia.

Indeed, it is virtually impossible for someone not born and raised in the USSR to appreciate how all-pervasive a figure Morozov is. Mikhalkov, who managed to condense the entire history of Pavlik Morozov into eight couplets, was not the only one to exploit this piece of Soviet history. Another famous Soviet poet, Stepan Stchipachev, wrote a long epic poem about Morozov. The composer V. Vitlin wrote a cantata for choir and symphony orchestra in praise of Morozov. There was even an opera written about him. Many of the greatest Soviet talents used their art to glorify the heroic deed of Morozov. Sergei Eisenstein and Isaac Babel worked on a film about him, and Maxim Gorky, in his speech to the first general meeting of the Union of Soviet Writers, called on the government to erect a monument to the hero.

As a consequence, everyone in the Soviet Union, young and old alike, knows about Pavlik Morozov. His portrait has appeared in art museums, on postcards, on matchbooks and postage stamps. Books, films, and canvases praised his courage. In many cities, he still stands in bronze, granite, or plaster, holding high the red banner. Schools were named after him. In special Pavlik Morozov Halls, children have been ceremoniously accepted into the Pioneers.* Statuettes of the young hero were awarded to the winners of sports competitions. Ships, libraries, city streets, collective farms, and national parks were named after Pavlik Morozov. His official title is Hero-Pioneer of the Soviet Union Number 001.

In 1982, on the fiftieth anniversary of the heroic death of Pavlik Morozov, the press called the boy "an ideological martyr." The place of his death was described as a sanctuary and the child as a saint. This was remarkable language for the atheistic Soviet press and revealed the theological nature

---

*Pioneers—a mandatory Communist organization for children from age ten to fourteen.

of Communist ideology. In a thousand years of Russian history, such glory had never been bestowed on a child.

At that time, I was still living in Moscow. I became curious about Pavlik Morozov's story and decided to investigate this child-hero.

I began by reading book after book. Remarkably, there was no agreement about even the simplest historical facts. For example, Pavlik Morozov's age at the time of his heroic death was reported as anything from eleven to fifteen. As for the village of his birth, Gerasimovka, sources placed it variously in the provinces of Tobolsk, Obsko-Irtishsk, and Omsk (in Siberia), as well as in Sverdlovsk in the Northern Urals. The photographs of the hero that were printed in various publications appeared to be of completely different people. In addition, I found as many as ten different persons identified as his murderer. Still another thing puzzled me. It was sometimes mentioned that Pavlik's younger brother, Fedya, also an informer, was murdered along with him, but it was never explained why he did not become a hero.

My surprise grew when I tried to obtain material from various state archives. There I always received the same answer: "We have no documents on Pavlik Morozov."

I did finally manage to locate Gerasimovka in Western Siberia. Boarding a train for the 36-hour ride, I headed for the boy-hero's home. But even there, in the Pavlik Morozov State Memorial Museum, there was not a single personal item, not a sheet from his school notebook, not one family relic to be found. I visited other Pavlik Morozov museums and instead of original documents found only sketches of the boy, books, and newspaper clippings. Relics from saints of a thousand years ago are sometimes still available, but I could find no traces of this twentieth-century saint. I began to wonder if the boy ever existed, other than as a fictional character in Soviet literature.

But one last bridge to the past remained: living witnesses. When I inquired at the museum in Gerasimovka whether I might meet with any of the witnesses, I encountered obvious resistance. "Tourists should not meet with villagers," objected the guide. "The peasants don't understand anything and might say the wrong thing. The museum guides have mapped out your tour so that you can visit the places of interest and then leave the village."

After being ushered on my official tour, however, I didn't leave. But everywhere I went I was accompanied by the director of the museum, so I couldn't talk to people or take photographs. I left the village for a nearby town and slipped back in a few days later. I quietly started going from house to house, avoiding the attention of officials. Even so, most of the villagers who were willing to talk with me at all were reluctant to answer direct questions.

In spite of these difficulties, the evidence of the eyewitnesses of the events in Gerasimovka gave me more information than I had thought possible. The official texts turned out to be rife with lies.

I met Elena Pozdnina, Morozov's schoolteacher. She had saved a photograph of her class from the year 1930, showing herself and Morozov among a few dozen village children, some of whom were still living in Gerasimovka. This seems to be the only authentic photograph of the boy, taken, according to Pozdnina, on the one occasion in Morozov's life when a traveling photographer visited the village. When I saw that unpublished photograph it became clear that the pictures of the boy in every encyclopedia, schoolbook, postcard, and postage stamp had been so routinely retouched that they had lost any resemblance to the original.

The villagers told me that mysterious events had occurred even after the murder of Pavlik Morozov. The house in which the boy and his family had lived burned to the ground. The villagers believed that it was arson, but it

The photograph of Elena Pozdnina's class, 1930. Pavel is in the back row, third from the right. Danila Morozov is to his left, holding a banner. Elena Pozdnina is at center.

was never investigated. And the grave of Pavlik Morozov and his brother had secretly been moved at night from one place to another.

Early in my investigations, I established three reliable facts. First, the legendary Pavlik Morozov had actually existed. Second, he really was killed. Third, his funeral took place on September 7, 1932, although it is not known when he was killed.

I realized that to find out what had happened nearly fifty years earlier, I would have to make haste. The surviving witnesses of the tragedy ranged in age from sixty-five to one hundred years. In just a few more years, most of them would be dead.

Private inquiries were always very hard to make in the Soviet Union. And since this was one of the untouchable subjects, any questioning of the standard history was risky. I had to make my inquiries cautiously.

I traveled to eleven cities to track down participants and witnesses of the story. I recorded the testimonies of Pavlik's former schoolmates and neighbors, two of his schoolteachers, his younger brother, Alexei, and even his mother, Tatyana Morozova. I also talked with one of the main actors in the tragedy, Pavel's cousin Ivan Potupchik, who was a secret informer in 1932. He later became an official employee of the regional OGPU. It was he who discovered the children's bodies.

Unfortunately, the official propaganda had done its work. Pavlik Morozov's biography had been greatly embellished during the fifty years since his death, and Pavlik's schoolmates remembered him mostly from reading about him. Even his eighty-year-old mother, who told me things about her son that had never been published, added, "Whatever is written in the books is correct." A classmate of Pavlik Morozov summarized the relationship between truth and myth this way: "I will tell you how it was, but before you publish it, you yourself must change it as necessary. You know how these things should be done." Even uneducated people knew the rules of the game.

None of the original journalists who were sent to Gerasimovka to write Morozov's story were still alive, but I was able to locate many of their families. In some cases family members allowed me to study their personal archives, including many unpublished documents. And later, in the homes of villagers who witnessed the bloody tragedy, I was shown documents, preserved by pure luck, that helped to fill in the gaps in human memory.

But the more I spoke to witnesses and studied personal archives, the wider became the gap between the child who looked younger than his age in the only extant photograph and the brave Pioneer who stood up to the enemies of socialism. After all the research, my image of Pavlik Morozov split in two. One was a country schoolboy; the other, a hero in bronze. The first one died on the day he was brutally slaughtered in the woods. The other, an immortal hero, was born that day—a model of the new Soviet man.

Maxim Gorky called Pavlik Morozov "a small miracle of our times," and Nikita Khrushchev, in his preface to the 1962 edition of the *Children's Encyclopedia*, called Pavlik Morozov an "immortal of this age." But the villagers primarily remembered the boy as a hooligan who smoked cigarettes and sang obscene songs. One of his teachers even thought he was mildly retarded, perhaps due to his mother's mental problems and his father's alcoholism. At the age of about twelve, he was still in first grade.

After extensive interviews and a thorough combing of the archives, I was able to piece together a reliable history of this child-hero.

He was named Pavel and called Pashka. In real life nobody ever called him Pavlik. This tender diminutive was not given to him until after his death and first appeared in an article in the Communist newspaper for

ЗВЕРСКОЕ УБИЙСТВО ПИОНЕРОВ МОРОЗОВЫХ
ОТВЕТИМ НА ВЫЛАЗКУ КУЛАЧЬЯ УДАРНОЙ БОРЬБОЙ ЗА ЗНАНИЯ

НАШ ОТВЕТ — СБОР ПОДАРКОВ ДЛЯ ДЕРЕВНИ

Убитый кулаками пионер Павлуша Морозов.

Ежедневно в редакцию поступают десятки протестов против зверского убийства шайкой кулаков двух пионеров-активистов. Со всех концов Советского союза приходят эти протесты. В них пионеры и школьники требуют расстрела кулаков — убийц пионеров.
Сотни протестов получены и выездной сессией суда, выехавшей на место злодейства — в Тавды.

ПРОЛЕТАРСКИЙ ОТПОР КУЛАЧЬЮ

ЗАМЕНИМ ПОГИБШИХ ТОВАРИЩЕЙ

ВЫСШУЮ МЕРУ — УБИЙЦАМ ПИОНЕРОВ

Top left: The first "photograph" of Pavlik Morozov that appeared in Pionerskaya Pravda ten days after his death seems to be based on the class photo taken two years earlier. In the original picture he wore a peasant shirt with a high collar, but Pionerskaya Pravda showed him with a bare neck. That would later change to a football jersey and then to a soldier's coat.

Top right: In 1932, an "improved" photo of Morozov was published in the book Collective Farm Children. A book entitled The New Way appeared in his hand.

Bottom: The second edition of the Greater Soviet Encyclopedia pictured Morozov in a military style cap, snow-white shirt, and Pioneer tie – a uniform introduced by Stalin after World War II. His facial expression had changed from gloomy to cheerful and determined.

МОРОЗОВ, Павлик (Павел 1918—32) — отважный пионер, самоотверженно боровшийся против кулаков своей деревни в период коллективизации; зверски убит кулаками.
Павлик Морозов родился в глухой деревне Герасимовке на Сев. Урале (ныне Тавдинский р-н Свердловской обл.) в бедняцкой семье. В селе М. был одним из лучших учеников, заслуженным среди товарищей, читал, обучил мать. Когда в селе создана пионерорганизация, М. был председателем отряда, вели активную борьбу против кулаков. М. разоблачил своего отца, бывшего в то время (1930) председателем сельского совета, но продавшего интересы нашей родины. Рассказав представителям партии о том, что его отец тайно выдавал кулакам ложные документы,

Morozov as he was shown by the Soviet media in the 1950s.

Morozov as he was shown in the 1970s.

children, *Pionerskaya Pravda*. From then on it was used by everyone.

The grandfather of the real Pavlik Morozov settled in Gerasimovka in 1910. Along with other settlers, he came from Byelorussia looking for available land. His son — Pavel's father, Trofim Morozov — was a soldier in the Red Army during the Civil War. By the beginning of the 1930s, he was chairman of the Village Council.

The exact date of Pavlik's birth is unknown. The Soviet encyclopedia says he was born on November 18, 1918, but the monument that stands on the site of his burned house gives his birthday as December 2, 1918. Even his mother could not remember his actual birthdate.

At first the Collectivization Plan did not affect so remote a place as Gerasimovka in the Ural administrative region. But in the early 1930s thousands of peasants from European Russia were exiled east to Siberia, and some of those exiles settled in Gerasimovka.

The regional authorities began to follow the example of the central government by arresting those who resisted the Collectivization Plan. It was a sad irony that at the same time exiles were arriving in Gerasimovka from elsewhere, residents of Gerasimovka were being exiled to even farther-flung parts of Siberia. One person's home became another person's place of exile.

At the time of this nationwide tragedy, which took millions of lives, a smaller but nonetheless dramatic event occurred in Gerasimovka.

Trofim Morozov left his wife, Tatyana, for another woman. This was an extraordinary thing to do at the time. Peasants commonly beat their wives, but they did not abandon them. Pavel, about age thirteen, was the oldest of four sons. The youngest was about four. Pavel's schoolmate Dimitri Prokopenko recalls, "When the father left the family, his responsibilities fell on Pavel's shoulders: to take care of a cow and a horse, to clean the barn, to collect firewood from the forest. For a while Trofim brought the family some food, but then he stopped. Pavel and his mother thought they could scare his father into returning. If Trofim had not left the family, there would have been neither denunciation nor murder nor heroism. But this is not for the press."

Kabina, another of Pavel's schoolteachers, believed that Tatyana Morozova encouraged her eldest son to complain about his father to the local OGPU. "She was an illiterate, ignorant woman," Kabina told me, "and she harassed her husband as much as she could after he left her. She taught Pavlik to inform, thinking that Trofim would get scared and return to the family."

But things turned out differently. Trofim was arrested, and OGPU officials instructed Tatyana and her son on how to testify at the trial. All the witnesses I spoke to agreed that the boy did not seem to understand what was going on.

Trofim Morozov was sentenced to ten years in jail and disappeared forever in the camps.* The court also ordered the confiscation of all his property. Since his second marriage was never legalized, his first family's property was seized. Tatyana and her four sons were left paupers. The villagers say that after the father's arrest, the Morozov children were constantly hungry and were grateful even for a piece of stale bread.

After being the center of attention as the prosecutor's key witness at his father's trial, Pavel became a regular informer. Survivors told me that he terrorized the whole village, spying on everybody. Having been a pawn in the family conflict, he became a pawn in the villagers' conflict with Soviet power over the demand that peasants become part of a collective farm, or *kolkhoz*.

---

*There is some indication that he was executed in a camp after his son's murder.

29

There was no mention at all of the heroism of Pavlik Morozov until after his murder. But once he was dead, *Pionerskaya Pravda* said: "Pavlik does not spare anybody...If he catches his own father doing wrong, he denounces him. If it is his grandfather, he denounces him as well. A kulak is hiding weapons — the courageous Pioneer exposes him. A villager sells in the black market — Pavlik reveals him for what he is. Pavlik was brought up by the Pioneers. He was growing up to be an outstanding Bolshevik." This very paragraph, without quotation marks, can be found in many books by different authors.

And here is what the witnesses have to say. His schoolmate Prokopenko: "Pavlik's heroism is terribly exaggerated. Pavlik was a punk, that's all. To be an informer, you know, is serious work. But he was just a miserable wretch. A louse." Zoya Kabanova, yet another of Pavel's schoolteachers: "Pavlik denounced his father, but that was all. He wasn't trying to support collectivization and he didn't understand anything about politics anyway." Lazar Baidakov, a relative of Pavel's who spent ten years in the gulag* in the 1930s, told me: "The boy himself did not play any serious role. As for why so much was made of him, you know perfectly well yourself."

Six months after his father's trial, Pashka Morozov was still unknown outside his village. But then he and his little brother Fedya were brutally slaughtered in the forest not far from their home, where they had gone to pick cranberries. Their bodies were discovered three days later by Ivan Potupchik, Pavel's cousin and an informer for the local OGPU, who called together all the villagers. He immediately declared that Pavel was a "hero-activist-Pioneer-Bolshevik" and had been slain by the enemies of the people, the kulaks.

In the personal archives of Pavel Salomein, the first journalist who was sent to Gerasimovka to cover the story, I

---

*gulag — The Soviet penal system under Stalin; Russian acronym for Chief Administration of Corrective Camps.

came across a number of remarkable documents given to him by the OGPU as supporting material for a book he was assigned to write about the hero. Among them was a copy of file number 374 from the regional OGPU's investigation into the murder of the Morozov brothers. It contained, among other things, a "Special OGPU Memo on the Question of Terror,"* listing the names of ten villagers from Gerasimovka who "on different occasions had been observed to demonstrate an anti-Soviet attitude." Right after Pavel's murder, all those on the list—Pavel's grandparents among them—were accused of murder, arrested, beaten, and sent to the OGPU investigation prison. Meanwhile, a rumor was deliberately spread in the area that all who opposed collectivization would be arrested. After that, the local OGPU reported to the central Party authorities in Moscow that a collective farm had finally been established in Gerasimovka, where the peasants had resisted it for a long time.

There was virtually no investigation of the murders. The brothers were buried, by OGPU order, even before the investigator arrived. It was never established exactly when they were killed, and no medical experts were ever consulted. Different documents differ on the number of wounds and the nature of the murder weapons. The main pieces of evidence were a bloody knife and some bloodstained clothes, which belonged to Pavel's cousin, Danila Morozov. The day before the children disappeared, Danila had slaughtered a calf for Pavel's mother, who took the meat to the market in a nearby town the next day. Danila made no attempt to hide the bloody knife and clothes, and no expert was brought in to establish whether the blood was human or animal.

No significance was given to the fact that none of the accused attempted to escape or to hide the "evidence,"

---

*Terror against peasants was an official policy of the Collectivization Plan.

even though they had three days to do so. Furthermore, the boys' bodies were left in plain sight near the road, but they weren't "discovered" until the third day, which may indicate that they were moved to that place three days after they were murdered.

Two months later, in the nearby city of Tavda, an open trial was held, which the press described as the "trial of all kulaks." The trial was publicized throughout the county. Four villagers, all said to be members of the "kulak anti-Soviet band," were found guilty of Pavel's murder and sentenced to death under Article 58-8 of the Criminal Code of the Russian Republic for "terrorism against representatives of the Soviet government." So it was that Pavel became a representative of the Soviet State after his death.

None of those sentenced confessed to the murder. They were all members of the Morozov family: Pavel's grandfather, Sergei Morozov, 81 years old; his grandmother, Ksenia, 80; his godfather and uncle, Arseni Kulukanov, 70; and Danila Morozov, 19, who had gone to school with Pavel. All four were executed immediately after the trial.

Also in Salomein's archives, I came across a mysterious unnumbered document of the Ural OGPU Secret Department. It was the minutes of the interrogation of Ivan Potupchik (who found Pavel's body) by an OGPU investigator, Spiridon Kartashev. Potupchik, according to the document, testified that the murder of Morozov had a "political character because Morozov Pavel was a Pioneer and an activist and spoke out in public meetings on behalf of the Soviet State and to expose the kulaks of Gerasimovka." Further on, the "minutes" give a detailed account of the heroic deeds of the Pioneer.

The most remarkable fact about this document is that it is dated September 4, 1932, two days before Ivan Potupchik is alleged to have found the bodies of the Morozov brothers. So it appears that while all the villagers, including Pavel's grandparents, were searching for the children, thinking that they had gotten lost in the woods, the OGPU agent and his informer had already described the murder and identified the ten individuals who would later be charged as kulaks and as Pavel Morozov's murderers.

This document made me suspect that Kartashev and Potupchik themselves killed the children. I spoke to both of them, and naturally they denied any connection with the murder. Today they are both dead, but we have the following information about them.

After the murders, Ivan Potupchik, who had formerly been an informer for the local OGPU, was officially employed in the mass executions of kulaks. Later, he was found guilty of the rape of a teenage girl and spent a short time in jail. After he was released, he was again employed by the OGPU, but received an assignment far from Gerasimovka.

Kartashev, an OGPU investigator, willingly spoke of his part in persecuting kulaks: "By my personal count, I shot thirty-seven people and sent many more to the camps. I know how to kill silently. Here's the secret: I tell them to open their mouth, and I shoot them close up. It sprays me with warm blood, like eau de cologne, and there's no sound. I know how to do this job—to kill."

But Potupchik and Kartashev and even those who organized the trial in Tavda and shot Morozov's relatives turned out to be small players. The campaign of terror was organized by much more highly placed individuals. A number of secret reports stamped "Terror, Series K" ("K" being short for kulaks) contained information about the "political murder" of Pavel Morozov and about the trial. These were prepared by the Tavda regional OGPU and then sent to Sverdlovsk, the capital of the Ural administrative region, and from there directly to the head of the Special Department of Stalin's personal secretariat, Alexander Poskrebyshev.

Stalin personally ordered that a monument to Morozov be erected at the entrance to Red Square* and presented Tatyana Morozova with a house in the Crimea, by the Black Sea. But there is no doubt that Stalin knew the whole truth.

Soon after the trial, Potupchik and Kartashev were sent away to work in the OGPU liquidation unit. Many of Morozov's remaining relatives were sent to camps. His younger brother, Alexei, who was ten years old when he testified at his grandparents' trial at Tavda, spent ten years in jail for "espionage" during the period of his dead brother's greatest glory. All the top Party officials of the Ural administrative region at the time of the trial were later purged.

Shortly after Stalin's death in 1953, an order came to officials in Gerasimovka to move the Morozov brothers' grave from the cemetery to a spot in front of the windows of the *kolkhoz* administration building. The operation took place in the middle of the night, with only the headlights of a car to illuminate the scene. KGB officials shoveled the contents of the old double grave into a wooden box, mixing the bones of the two brothers together. They dug a deep hole, laid the box in it, and poured six feet of concrete on top of it. Erection of a monument completed the job. Any further exhumation became impossible.

Meanwhile, Pavlik Morozov had become a legend. He was the model of the "New Soviet Man." The real village boy had been superseded by the official hero. "He deserved the honorable name of Communist that he carried," *Pionerskaya Pravda* wrote of Morozov, even though there were no Communist Party members in the village at that time, not to mention that Pavel was too young to be one. He was also called "a deserving ward of the Lenin

---

*Later Stalin changed his mind and ordered the monument to be placed on a small Moscow street named after Morozov.

Tatyana Morozova, Morozov's mother.

Bronze monument to Pavlik Morozov in the center of Moscow.

Daily morning ritual: children put a red pioneer tie on a plaster bust of Morozov (photograph from a propaganda booklet).

Komsomol,"* although a chapter of the Komsomol was not formed in Gerasimovka until after Pavel's death. In fact, there was no Pioneer chapter there either. Matrena Korolkova, Pavel's schoolmate, said, "About him being a Pioneer, the truth is they just wanted that to be the case." Elena Pozdnina, told me, "No, Pavel Morozov was not a Pioneer. But you must understand: To make a good hero he had to be a Pioneer."

In Salomein's personal notes, I found this unpublished comment: "To be historically correct, Pavlik Morozov not only never wore a Pioneer tie, but never even saw one."

Another piece of the Morozov myth was created in the early 1950s, during the campaign against "cosmopolitanism," or Western influence and the "bourgeois liberal values" associated with it. The press started calling Morozov "a Russian boy." Soviet Hero Number One *had* to be Russian. In actual fact, Morozov and all the rest of the villagers were Byelorussian.

The practice of people's informing on each other had begun in Lenin's time. Some of Lenin's early comrades recalled that he asked them to write anonymous denunciations of his political adversaries. As General Secretary of the Communist Party, Stalin routinely eavesdropped on his colleagues with a secret listening device.

It was Lenin who appointed Stalin head of the Worker-Peasant Inspection Commission, which collected compromising information about State employees. Even earlier, Stalin had begun to use the OGPU apparatus to collect compromising information, both genuine and concocted, about people who interfered with his plans. The informer system became Stalin's practical instrument for destroying

---

*Komsomol—Young Communist League, a Communist organization for youths from late adolescence to age 28.

his adversaries and consolidating his own position. And for his subordinates, informing was a way to prove their loyalty, to gain their leader's favor, and to further their careers.

The new Soviet citizen had a duty to inform on his fellow citizens. In this way he demonstrated his loyalty to the great goal of socialism, in which many informers sincerely believed. And there were those who apparantly enjoyed being informers and participated enthusiastically in the denunciation campaign.

Under Stalin's direction, a State agency for the collection of denunciations was formed, a nationwide ear called the Complaint Bureau. The information gathered by the Complaint Bureau was used by the Prosecutor's office and the OGPU.

The campaign to encourage mass denunciations was carried out with great enthusiasm. Denunciations became a regular feature of the Soviet press. A newspaper's condemnation was almost as powerful as a court's sentence. The Deputy People's Commissar of Education, Nadezhda Krupskaya (Lenin's widow), instructed children to "be observant at all times in order to help the Party eradicate its enemies." Hundreds of new Morozovs were praised in the press and were rewarded for their good work by a trip to Artek, a prestigious Pioneer summer camp on the Black Sea.

Feeling helpless in the face of this national tide of surveillance, people sometimes took the law into their own hands. During the years of Stalin's terror, there were at least fifty-six reported murders of young informers. Misguided by their teachers, these children, like their model, Morozov, were the victims of a political struggle they were too young to understand.

It seems clear that Morozov became a hero because just such a hero was needed to represent Stalin's political campaign, one that would pave the way for the mass purges and repressions of the 1930s, 1940s, and 1950s. The Soviet propaganda apparatus needed a model of a comrade whose first and last loyalty was to the Party.

It was Lenin's goal "to improve the mass of human material damaged by centuries of slavery." Stalin simplified the task by liquidating the "damaged material." Stalin saw the old morality as the main obstacle to achieving the goals of communism, and any vestiges of it had to be wiped out.

Morozov's generation, born after the Revolution, was the one to carry out Stalin's plans. These post-Revolutionary young people grew up without traditional moral values. They knew no social system but communism, and they were easily influenced by government propaganda. Anatoly Lunacharsky, the People's Commissar of Education from 1917 until 1929, explained the principles of Bolshevik education: "Since our state is a military dictatorship, we cannot follow the humanitarian criteria that used to be the foundation of our culture. To practice kindness in our present situation is treason. We must uproot our enemies before we can be kind."

For more than fifty years, Soviet children were taught to keep a sharp eye out for enemies of the people, even among their neighbors and family members. A young Komsomol leader, A. Ksoarev, wrote in *Pravda*, "We do not share a common morality with the rest of mankind...For us, morality is that which builds Socialism."

Moved by this kind of "morality," Stalin and his government easily converted millions of living people into corpses. But in the case Pavlik Morozov, a corpse was converted into a living symbol. Through the power of this legend, Stalin raised up an army of Morozov imitators, and the myth became a reality of Soviet life.

Translated from the Russian by
Sonia Melnikova and Susan Moon

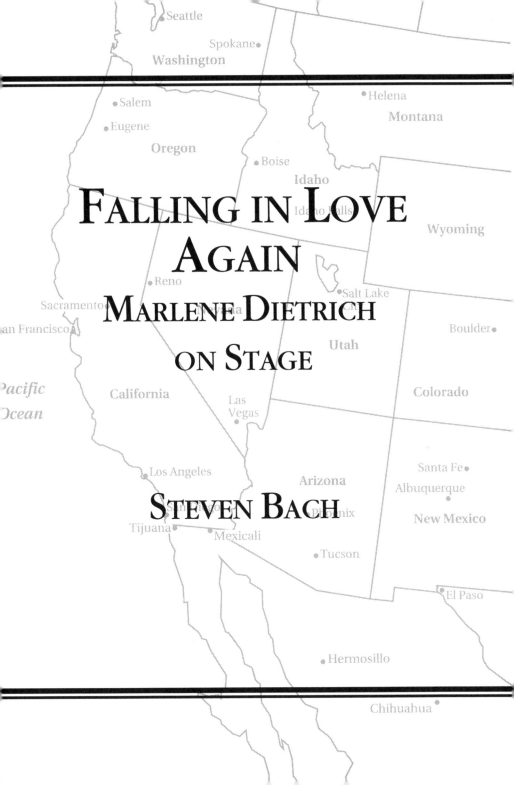

Falling in Love Again

Again

Marlene Dietrich

on Stage

Steven Bach

© Jerry Bauer

Steven Bach was born in Pocatello, Idaho. He received his bachelor's and master's degrees at Northwestern University and then continued his studies at the Sorbonne in Paris, France, and the University of Southern California.

Mr. Bach taught American literature before entering show business as a press agent. He later worked as assistant to the artistic director for the Mark Taper Forum in Los Angeles. Mr. Bach subsequently became a film producer and eventually head of worldwide production for United Artists. He was involved in the making of dozens of films including *Sleuth*, *The French Lieutenant's Woman*, *Raging Bull*, and *Manhattan*. He is the author of *Final Cut: Dreams and Disaster in the Making of Heaven's Gate* and most recently *Marlene Dietrich: Life and Legend*.

Mr. Bach divides his time between the United States and Europe.

"Somebody moved the microphone," she said.

She said it in that voice Hemingway wrote "could break your heart," but that was not its aim at the moment. There was an insistence in it now that sounded not from emphasis, but from reserve—a hush almost overridden by the bustle of adjusting chairs and instrument cases clicking open and biting shut somewhere on the stage behind her. There was the faintest break in this rustle of busy background as another voice, this one male, said, "Sorry?"

"Somebody moved the microphone," she repeated, as calmly as before, as quietly.

"Fellas, *please*," said the man. Scraps of sound on the stage scudded away and shivered to silence. "I don't get it, Marlene," he said.

"Somebody moved the microphone while we were at lunch." She colored the words with the faintest hue of authority—not with volume, but with shading, modulation, a veil. "Moving the microphone is nightclubs. This is not nightclubs. This is *theater.* This is *concerts.*"

Her final word resonated in silence.

Then, "Right, Marlene," the man said, and dutifully turned to the others, his voice flat: "No touching the mike, okay, fellas?" just as if they had not been there to hear it for themselves.

"Thank you, Burt," said the break-your-heart voice at the precise instant a squeal ran through the sound system, as if some sibilant gremlin in the circuitry were confirming her point.

Silence. Then the slash of a downbeat.

A song began.

"I can't give you anything but love, Baby..."

*   *   *

The screech of the speaker pierced the offices of the Ahmanson Theater, on the stage of which the microphone had been moved. Through one of those design oversights that in the age of the Habsburgs had prompted architects' suicides-of-honor, the 2071-seat Ahmanson, part of the giant Music Center complex in downtown Los Angeles, had been built without administrative offices. The more modest, mostly more adventurous Mark Taper Forum just steps away, managed by the same organization, turned out to have neither offices nor even a proper backstage in which to stow the stuff of artifice.

Though such standard necessities had been overlooked, the architects had shrewdly enough decreed a bar for each of the Ahmanson's three levels of seating. Each bar was equipped with speakers connected to the stage sound system to alert patrons and bartenders that something was about to begin or end.

When it was pointed out that no offices existed in either of the multimillion-dollar edifices, the Ahmanson's third-floor bar was quickly and neatly converted to windowless cubicles for the staffs of both theaters. Work supplies were stored in cabinets designed to hold champagne and crystal behind doors with locks, from which dangled tiny keys. They sometimes swayed, giving workers visible evidence that somewhere in the windowed world a seismic event was occurring.

Seismic events of moment to theater people are often of minor geologic magnitude, like the moving of a microphone. It was to track such occurrences that the speaker system from the stage to the converted bar had been switched on that morning, allowing staffs to eavesdrop on the rehearsal below in clandestine privacy.

It was, in fact, the first time in anyone's memory that the speaker system had been turned on. While theater people are notoriously curious, they can also be blasé to the bone, and in this case they had work to do. Activation of the sound system was less a tribute to the performer on stage—at first, anyway—than due to the persistence of the newly hired assistant to the creative director. This newcomer worked at a script-laden table next to the duplicating machine, which happened to be placed directly beneath the speakers and the switches that controlled them. The switches that controlled *him* were mostly out of sight.

There were a dozen or so staff members, preparing productions, rejecting scripts, conducting auditions, planning publicity, signing up subscribers. They ran the theatrical gamut: experience-toughened pros from New York who had Seen It All, to frighteningly dedicated (and ambitious) newcomers right out of drama school. Some were twenty-five going on fifty; some were fifty going on nerves and little else. But they shared a common and ageless affliction: Their veins, whether hardened with disillusion or flexibly free to experience Everything, were chock full of greasepaint. They were (or wanted to be) Theater People, and every ear, dimmed by time or still wet-behind with innocence, was being firmly bent by a sixty-six-year-old woman who was assuring them in a cognac voice that there was nothing she could give them "*...but love, Baby.*"

Everybody knew the words and tune of the old chestnut purring now through the speakers from the stage, but to their slowly growing surprise twenty-six musicians and a German grandmother were making it sound freshly minted. She was slurring it and nudging it in its durable ribs and grinning through the words. There was smoke in that voice, faint echoes of decades: Berlin in the twenties; Hollywood in the thirties; locales exotic and tragic and battlefields in a dozen countries in the forties. But these echoes were muted now, hidden behind humor. She was making them forget all that, so the Now could pierce—or displace—the Then; promising "*diamond bracelets Woolworth doesn't sell,*" every facet flawless, glinting in swing.

And then—suddenly—she wasn't promising anything anymore. She had stopped in mid-phrase, and it took conductor and orchestra several moments to realize this and wind down in a discordant blare, like a carousel whose gears have slipped and is grinding to a crazy, whimpering halt.

Faces around the office speaker exchanged glances as silence loomed and broadened.

"What is it, Marlene?" asked the man—Burt Bacharach, to be sure, her arranger, conductor, and accompanist from 1955 to 1964, who had agreed to return for just this one concert in 1968, four years after a decade that had ended in Edinburgh.

"The electric guitars," she replied.

"What about them?" Bacharach didn't seem alarmed or even much interested.

"One of them is too loud," she said, with the quiet confidence of a radar technician.

"They're not too loud, Marlene. Let's keep going."

"*One* of them is too loud," she repeated, the decibels diminishing as if in deference, but calibrated with hairline exactness to control.

There was a pause before Bacharach yielded. "Okay, fellas. *Readings.*" Then another pause. "Fred?"

"She's right, Burt," said Fred, faint but clear. "Must've accidentally kicked it up."

"Well, kick it down," ordered Bacharach tightly. Then a beat. "Okay, Marlene?"

"Thank you, Burt," she said, and within a rhythmic blink was again promising—and delivering—"*the only thing I've plenty of, Baby...*"

It was Theater, performed for an audience of twenty-six local musicians to whom she had her back on that stage. They were mostly studio musicians, among the best in the world (she had reason to know), but often casual by

conditioning, by "cool." Expert technicians, flawlessly but perhaps indifferently doing a gig. They would accompany her for two weeks, following four days of eight-hour rehearsals, of which this was the first for them, the thousandth for her.

"This is not nightclubs," she had said. "This is *theater.* This is *concerts,*" and with a minor *coup de théâtre*, standards had been posted. Twenty-six adult professionals— and even a famous composer—had been informed that this was no gig. They were to give her, as she was to give her audience, "*all those things you've always pined for...,*" bar by bar, beat by beat, purr by purr.

Maybe those twenty-six union men sensed something special about this concert. Maybe the reason Bacharach had consented to come back briefly from his composing and his films. Maybe a heightened tension, an awareness that this was, as Berlin had been in 1960—and Bacharach had been there, too—a kind of homecoming where there was no longer any home; a return to the past designed to convey only the present.

Maybe this theater, this concert, this town and audience, would be different from London or Paris or Rio or Warsaw or Moscow or even Broadway. This stage on which she stood was in the heart of a company town that could be cruel and callous or—even worse—indifferent. It was capital to an industry whose current managers would be there Friday night, "suits" for whom she was mostly a memory or a scrapbook of irrelevant stills, but of whose history she was an immutable part, a legendary icon; and they were people who respected no history older than yesterday's grosses.

Maybe that was why on this first day of rehearsal—as the voice insinuated itself again and again around rhythms already perfect—through the elegance of the phrasings, the shimmer of the orchestrations, shone something else: the glint not of glamour, but of honed steel; a legend's determination to endure.

Neither Dietrich, nor Bacharach, nor the orchestra was aware of the surreptitious surveillance of their rehearsal going on far above their heads. But by the second morning of run-throughs, the theater administration was and clamped down fast. The obvious slowing in workday activity was not the point: It was as if Babe Ruth had stopped off for a little batting practice and the home team was allowed to climb the fence for a look. This much seemed harmless, maybe even instructive, good for morale.

Lost time could be made up, *would* be, but a breached contract was not so easily repaired; Miss Dietrich's producer (herself) had strictly forbidden observation of her rehearsals, and the auditorium had been placed under contractual quarantine. Technically, perhaps, nothing was being breached but faith. The theater itself was merely being booked for her engagement, and she herself was responsible for every aspect of its presentation, from posters and lighting to liability insurance and costs of the musicians and the union dues. She therefore had the right to demand and to get what she demanded. However pleasurable or even edifying electronic eavesdropping might be, it was at the expense of a guaranteed privacy, and somehow deemed not quite "professional."

The only member of the staff inconvenienced in any real way didn't even work on the third floor, and thus escaped the grumble following the speaker-system ban. This was the Ahmanson's stage manager, whose office was situated (another architectural mystery) below the orchestra floor, reachable only by trekking through the auditorium.

This grizzled and unflappable professional solved his problem simply by arriving before Dietrich and her entourage started to work around ten o'clock each morning, and leaving after they had finished, about six. What he did between ten and six was anybody's guess and nobody's business, for with Dietrich in temporary charge of his theater, he had no current responsibilities beyond keeping the lights on and himself out of sight.

On the third floor, however, things began to simmer with a sense of deprivation. The theater publicity manager, Peg, tried to assuage these feelings by promising to get press passes for those who were least well paid or whose noses were most out of joint. Even this normally routine accommodation was problematic, however, for press tickets were all but gone and "paper" — free tickets to fill empty seats — was forbidden by the Dietrich contract.

Despite the restrictions, later that day the office newcomer turned away from the photocopier, put down whatever he was duplicating, and made for the corridor.

"Let it happen," publicity Peg called after him.

He slipped through the door into the warm, floating rhythms of "Honeysuckle Rose" and threw caution to impulsive, even dangerous winds by stealing into the last row of the top balcony.

He was relieved to find the theater dark except for work lights on stage, but he hunched down in the first seat to avoid the remote possibility of being seen from the stage.

"Honeysuckle Rose" was snapping and slinking down there, with a swagger suggesting that Lola Lola from "The Blue Angel" had lightened up her act and linked arms with Fats Waller to saunter down Broadway. What riveted his attention was not the elegant swing, or the silk of the orchestration, but the pale blonde figure, barely swaying before the microphone. Somehow he had expected feathers and spangles and lighting that enhanced and concealed. Instead of plumes, she wore a simple daytime suit in the glare of naked bulbs, and the image was so contemporary, so workaday, that questions of age and the past became irrelevant.

The almost imperceptible sway was accompanied by the occasional flick of a finger or the turn of a wrist suggesting pleasure at toying with the swing. It seemed to him the most elegant economy of effect he had ever seen. The low voice flowed through the theater like amber candy, bubbling with amusement at the improbability of turning a Harlem evergreen into blonde velvet. He wasn't close enough to see the grin or the wink, but they were there to hear in the voice—which, for the second time in as many days, abruptly stopped.

Far below, at about the tenth row of orchestra seats, the husky, squat figure of the Taper's stage manager was suddenly visible, clanking his nuts and bolts across the forbidden auditorium on the only path to the office of the Ahmanson's stage manager below. Even he did not fail to hear an entire orchestra grind to a halt, and his stride faltered. He turned to the stage, to the pale blonde saber who stood there straight and silent and shining sharp. He began hoarsely to explain himself. His voice echoed in the empty theater, and his self-assurance withered as he found himself addressing twenty-six musicians and a conductor, for the lady—no grins or winks now—had vanished.

This should have been a clear cue for the crouching witness to depart the top balcony while the departing was good, but he had a streak of pettiness and remained, relishing the discomfort into which the intruder had fallen a couple of thousand seats below. His words were having no effect, for Burt Bacharach stood at his piano not even listening. He was looking into the wings where Dietrich had disappeared. The stage technician's voice seemed to dribble away, and he backed down the aisle, clanking much less than before, and did his own vanishing act.

As soon as he was gone, Dietrich marched back on stage and regarded Bacharach in silence for a moment as if they shared unspeakable burdens. Even from the last row of the top balcony it was possible to see that not a muscle moved anywhere on stage. Then Dietrich turned to her conductor and in that silken voice, that satin scabbard for the steel within, said, "Let's do some lights."

She pivoted back to face the auditorium, and her observer in the balcony had the impression she was staring directly at him as he crouched there guiltily. Instead, the voice called out—projecting strongly now—to someone unseen, somewhere in the theater. "Joe?"

"Ready," said Joe, from somewhere.

"Try to hit me here," she said, positioning herself again squarely before the microphone, "for the end of 'Honeysuckle.' Full up."

She stood unmoving as lights began to play. She waited patiently, then, "There, there, that's it," though no one on stage—or in the last row of the balcony—could tell how she knew.

"At the end I do the two steps..." She paused and frowned. "This stage is too deep...*three*. I'll do three steps back—applause, applause, then three to my right for the bow...no, *two*," she said, adjusting her movements to the shape and dimensions of the stage. "Gold, please. Not the pink."

She moved briskly as she talked, going through her moves, pausing for light adjustments in the daytime suit and low-heeled shoes. She raised her chin slightly, as if acknowledging applause in the empty theater, paused, called out, "Too hot. *Here*." Her palm pressed against her temple. An adjustment was made in the light, her skin tested it again, and she pronounced it "Fine," moving into another pattern of movements, pausing for settings of lights her pale skin could seemingly measure, not unaware that an orchestra was watching this display of sensitivity not merely to light, but to the minutest details of stagecraft.

"Now 'Where Have All the Flowers Gone?,'" she said to Joe, and resumed her position before the microphone, crossing her arms behind her back. The pinks and golds and blues disappeared, and she stood there in street make-up, her face haloed by pale hair pulled back sharp from her forehead and held in place by a ribbon across the crown, a candle flame, steady, unwavering.

"More," she told Joe. "A little higher," and—even from the top balcony—drama formed, dependent on nothing more than a light and facial planes that softened and glowed against the immense, dark stage. She stood there like an exclamation point against the darkness.

It was not a question of beauty. Not "mere" beauty, anyway, the assistant thought, not of any conventional kind. It was that, all right, but something beyond that. It was what she had said it was: Theater, but of no kind he had seen or experienced before.

Just then, another light appeared, a slice of it to his left. Bob, the publicity-trainee, peered into the balcony and whispered, "Get the hell out of there."

The assistant stepped reluctantly into the corridor. "Guess who just got fired?" Bob asked, grinning.

"By whom?" asked the newcomer, that candle flame still burning.

"The Great White Bureaucrat," Bob said. "On the telephone from New York. That Kraut lady don't fool around."

"New York? If the beloved leader isn't here..."

The speakers went back on.

The third day of rehearsals began with more stage directions, more light settings, more polishing and honing of movement and music in a drive to perfection.

"Then I'll say, 'And here's a song from "The Blue Angel,"'" the voice murmured through the speakers, "and someone will begin to applaud and I'll say 'No, no, it's not *that* one,' and then someone will call out 'Lola'..."

"She must have 'plants' in the audience," said Peg knowingly.

"Or if no one does—this is Hollywood, after all, where memories are short," came the voice with an edge and a smile, "I'll tell them myself—'Lola'—and then move here..."

The musical repertoire had broadened over the hours of rehearsal, though it was still pieces of a mosaic, rather than a finished product. French and German rubbed shoulders with Tin Pan Alley and Hollywood, and there was a relentless repetition as each number in whatever language or mood was polished to a perfection that perhaps no ear but its singer's could detect.

No violin or strum of bass viol strings, no grace note of piano or clarinet, no shadow or beam of light was exempt from her attention, her correction. She drove the lights and shadows and sounds as she drove herself, tirelessly, without complaint or drama. She exhausted every opportunity for improvement, every musician on that stage, everything but her apparently inexhaustible self.

As the newcomer, alone or with others, watched this force of nature disguised in smart but simple street clothes as just a person, he began to sense the pattern of the mosaic she was constructing.

He, like the rest, had expected a parade of "Dietrich's Greatest Hits": Lola Lola from "The Blue Angel," segueing to Frenchy from "Destry Rides Again," or Shanghai Lily alighting from her "Express" in veils and black feathers. Instead he was getting none of them, or all of them, but subtly altered, matured, crossed and mixed, simplified and deepened. They were there, but something more was too. She dared to strive for the perfection that conceals art while revealing her mastery of every trick of artifice at her disposal, and though she did so with the energy of a tank corps, was making it look easy.

And still the mosaic was incomplete. The drive for perfection concealed the final pattern. It was like observing the most perfect of precision watchworks without knowing the time.

*   *   *

On the fourth and final day of rehearsals the theater "suit" returned from New York. There were no more stealthy trips to the upper balcony, no crowding around the speakers; just an impatient suspense as to how and if she were pulling the pieces together. It wasn't just "I Can't Give You Anything But Love, Baby" and "Honeysuckle Rose," with their bright impertinence; but "La Vie En Rose," and its melancholy; and "Frag Nicht Warum Ich Gehe," with its fatalistic farewell to lost love. Or the one they had never heard before, the one from Israel that she sang like a lioness in some wilderness. And "Lili Marlene," cloudy with the smoke of battlefields, and "Where Have All the Flowers Gone?," hurled at the rows of empty seats like an accusation from an angry goddess.

Finally, late in the fourth day, the coast cleared. The speakers were switched back on in time to hear Bacharach thank his musicians and announce that rehearsals were over. The expected snap and click of instrument cases and the hubbub of small talk didn't happen. Silence lingered on the speakers until broken by a voice that was hushed, but heavy as the world.

"All right," she said. "All right. Burt says rehearsals are over, it's time to stop, time to go, and Burt knows. He knows your union rules and your own rules; he knows your freeways and your lawn sprinklers and your swimming pools and your televisions, your standards and your aspirations." The voice grew even quieter, more somber than it had ever sounded in any film, on any recording. "And so you must go home to your little wives in your little houses in the hills or the San Fernando Valley. I am prepared and willing to stay here all night. All night and all tomorrow, too. To get it right. To justify this thing we are doing, this act of theater. But no. Your pools and martinis and television sets and wives are waiting, so never mind. Never mind that we are not ready for them. But go. Go home to Burbank or Encino or Covina...and relax. And as you do, think that we open tomorrow night, and that tomorrow night will be..." her voice hushed to near inaudibility, "...a disaster."

Footsteps carried her off the stage.

Finally Bacharach said, "That's it," and gathered his music. The stage cleared without another word.

The day of predicted disaster began in calm and quiet, as there was no rehearsal on which to eavesdrop. There was another calm, lingering from Dietrich's final words to her orchestra. No earthquake, no tantrum: just a glacial floe, a quiet avalanche of reproach.

Tasks neglected since Monday were resumed or completed. There were no leftover press passes, as it turned out, nor unsold tickets at the box office, so none of the staff would be attending the premiere performance. At day's end the pros and the tyros extended weekend wishes to each other and joined the crush on the crowded freeways home.

The Taper's new creative assistant did so in a subdued silence, unbroken by the usual chatter of his car radio. When he arrived at his tiny apartment, he showered, shaved, brushed and donned his one suit and best tie, got back into his third-hand car to drive to the corner market, where he bought a bottle of California champagne, and then guided himself back to the freeway, back to the Music Center.

He parked in the underground cavern, took the escalator to the plaza as he did each day, and with work keys let himself into the offices, now deserted.

He set the champagne on the table next to the duplicating machine, retrieved a coffee cup from an overhead shelf, and stepped into the windowed third-floor lobby to watch the traffic patterns around the complex, just as the fountains of the Department of Water and Power began to play and lights came on across the dusky, endless sprawl. City of the Angels.

The off-ramps of the freeways were clogging now, and limousines crawled around the block, pausing to permit gowns and black-ties to exit and stroll across the plaza to the theater. Who were they? he wondered. What were they coming to see? He returned to the office.

He switched on the speakers to the stage and listened to the babble of that elite: voyeurs with no investment in this opening but the price of a ticket. He wondered at his own investment and, oddly, could not calculate it. Or reason why he had one.

He pushed the plastic cork from the bottle of champagne and filled his coffee cup. As the audience grew silent and the music began on the speaker system, he sipped and listened. The orchestra blared a few bars of "Falling in Love Again" as if it were an anthem, and applause drowned out the music before that blonde velvet began to croon, "*I can't give you anything but love, Baby...*"

He had heard it a hundred times that week and suddenly knew he had not heard it at all. There was a melting warmth to the voice, an intimate, ingratiating shrug that said, "See how easy this is?," and the orchestra was a seamless, gliding thing that followed the voice as if on a leash.

He put down his cup, drawn by the voice out of the office and down the corridor, into the narrow standing space just inside the balcony. It was all working now, he saw. Theater in progress. Far below, the candle flame glowing, making magic. She was wearing what looked like liquid stars poured over a perfect body, and her hair swayed and swirled like a golden curtain when she flung her head in delight or lowered it in the deep bow with which she received homage the audience hadn't known it was going to give.

It wasn't a legend down there, some waxworks figure of

nostalgia, but a Presence, an actress leading her audience through a range of moods and personality they hadn't guessed were there. She was giving them the legend, of course, but playing with it, and on it, ringing changes, letting them know she had gone beyond it, perhaps, always more than that streamlined icon of erotic sophistication they had come to remember. It was a display of majesty and variety, custom so elegant it could not stale, and the seeming ease conveyed to those thousands of eyes in whose glow she basked that all of it was inevitable and, maybe, indestructible.

The assistant had heard each word, each note, each prediction of movement and lighting and audience response. He knew nothing had been left to chance or accident, but still felt caught up in the web of some sorcery, some enchantment, and he realized at last what made it work. It wasn't "Lola Lola" he watched, or "Frenchy," or any of the other images he knew: this was Dietrich's Dietrich, the *Ding an sich*, the essence of whatever she was or wanted them to believe she was, or maybe what *she* wanted to believe she was. With that she overwhelmed and obliterated the past. There was only Now, diamond-dusted and glowing like a moon. Ageless and fleeting and forever, in that place that Time can't reach.

The "disaster" was widely reviewed, of course. The following Monday, now that the auditorium was no longer rehearsal ground, the assistant crossed the rows of empty seats on his way to the Ahmanson stage manager's office, scripts for technical breakdown under his arm. As he walked he read the town's most important review, the one in the *Los Angeles Times*. "This timeless sorceress," he read, "sang, or performed, or did whatever it was she did and gave you gooseflesh..."

He interrupted his reading to descend the stairs to the stage manager's office. The old pro sat feet crossed at the ankles on his desk, a steaming cup of coffee at his lips.

"Yeah?" he said.

"Scripts," said the younger man, handing them to him.

"These are for the Taper," the stage manager said, handing them back after the briefest glance.

"Yes, but—"

"He'll be back. It was only a fake firing. Just to make a point, just for effect, just for the week." The gray-haired man tugged at his coffee cup and let his eyes wander to the tape recorder on his desk. He heaved his feet from the desktop, grunted, and punched a button on the machine. The reels began to turn and the basement office filled with the voice Hemingway said could break your heart.

"And then I'll say, 'And here's a song from "The Blue Angel,"' and someone will begin to applaud and then I'll say 'No, no, it's not *that* one...'"

The stage manager switched the machine off and leaned heavily on the desktop. "The speaker system feeds down here, too, you know," he said. "All four days of it is there on tape. Every word. All the sweat. You ever want to hear it, come on down."

"But why?" asked the assistant.

The older man sipped his coffee, then nodded to the newspaper open to the review in the assistant's hand. "Because it'll be proof of what happened and how you get to be a star and how you get to *stay* a star."

I understood. Or thought I did. And went back to work.

ALEKSANDR
SOLZHENITSYN
BEYOND ETIQUETTE

TOM WOLFE

Tom Wolfe was born in Richmond, Virginia. He graduated from Washington and Lee University and received a doctorate in American Studies from Yale University.

Mr. Wolfe was a reporter for the *Washington Post*, the *New York Herald Tribune*, and the *Springfield Union*. His writing has also appeared in *New York* magazine, *Esquire*, and *Harper's*.

Mr. Wolfe is the author of several bestsellers, including *The Bonfire of the Vanities*, *The Electric Kool-Aid Acid Test*, and *Radical Chic and Mau-Mauing the Flak Catchers*. *The Painted Word*, his book on modern art, received a special citation from the National Sculpture Society. In 1979, he published *The Right Stuff*, which won the American Book Award for general nonfiction. Mr. Wolfe was the recipient of the Harold D. Vursell Memorial Award from the American Academy and Institute of Arts and Letters in 1980. That same year he received the Columbia Journalism Award for distinguished service in the field of journalism.

Mr. Wolfe lives in New York City.

*A*leksandr Solzhenitsyn was born in 1918 in Kislovodsk,
Russia. He studied mathematics and physics at Rostov
University and took correspondence courses at the Moscow
Institute of History, Philosophy, and Literature. He joined the
Army in 1941, graduated from Artillery School in 1942, and
served as an artillery battery commander at the front until 1945.
He was twice decorated for his military service.

In 1945 Mr. Solzhenitsyn was arrested by the Soviet armed
forces counterintelligence agency for the "crime" of making
derogatory comments about Joseph Stalin in a letter to a friend.
He was sentenced to eight years' imprisonment in a labor camp
and to permanent internal exile in Siberia. In 1956, he was
released from exile as a result of political reforms. He began to
teach at a high school and continued to write. In 1962, the year
he was allowed to publish One Day in the Life of Ivan
Denisovich, he was admitted to membership in the Union of
Soviet Writers. He was expelled from the Union in 1969 and
was awarded the Nobel Prize for Literature in 1970. In 1974 he
was charged with treason, stripped of his Soviet citizenship, and
flown against his will to West Germany. Two years later he and
his family emigrated to the United States.

The following is the text of a speech delivered in honor of
Aleksandr Solzhenitsyn on the occasion of his being awarded the
Literary Award of the National Arts Club, January 19, 1993.

The story of the American literary community's reaction to
the arrival of Aleksandr Solzhenitsyn in the United States
is a droll chapter in the human comedy that might be
entitled *Many Vanities and Their Wounds*. But it is also an
important part of the intellectual history of the last part of
the twentieth century and in an oblique way a measure of
Solzhenitsyn's extraordinary achievement.

In the United States we first heard the name Aleksandr

Solzhenitsyn in 1962 when Nikita Khrushchev [premier of the Soviet Union] in effect put his arm around Solzhenitsyn and said, "Yes, you can publish your novella *One Day in the Life of Ivan Denisovich*, because, yes, these things did happen. Concentration camps such as you describe did exist, and it was all the fault of the man who led socialism astray, Joseph Stalin."

In the short run this was a rather shrewd move by Khrushchev and the Communist leadership, who needed to deflate the enormous presence of Stalin's ghost. In the long run it was a fatal mistake. In *The Oak and the Calf*, Solzhenitsyn describes how in the years after the publication of *One Day in the Life of Ivan Denisovich* the leadership continued to put its arms around him, saying, "Well, now that you have taken care of this regrettable episode in our past, you'll be moving on to other things, won't you?" In fact he moved on to *The First Circle* and to *Cancer Ward*, restating in much larger terms the atrocities that had been perpetrated in the name of socialism and Marxism in the Soviet Union. Not only that, he became an openly outspoken dissenter against the Soviet regime in 1967. In 1970 he was awarded the Nobel Prize in literature and declined to go to Stockholm to receive the award for fear he would not be allowed to return to the Soviet Union.

The Soviet leaders by this time realized that they had big trouble on their hands. They did not realize, however, just how big it was soon to become. In 1973, the first volume of *The Gulag Archipelago* was smuggled out of the Soviet Union and published in France. This was a stunning event. It informed the world for the first time of the existence of a network of concentration camps from one end of the Soviet Union to the other that were the underpinning of the country's entire political and economic system. Into this "sewage disposal system," as Solzhenitsyn called it, tens of millions of human beings had been funneled and had perished. I say, "informed the world"; I should say, "made the world believe at last." Others had informed the world of the existence of the gulag. The English historian Robert Conquest had written about it in detail. But his accounts were based upon the testimony of refugees. And the testimony of refugees is simply not believed. I'm not sure why this is true, but refugees are not believed. Solzhenitsyn was not a refugee. He refused to be one, refused to leave the country if he could possibly avoid it. Also, there was no way the Soviet leadership could now gainsay his testimony. After all, the regime itself had already validated the accuracy of his statements, from Khrushchev on down.

What this meant was that it became, in the West in any case, no longer possible to believe in communism or in Marxism. It became an absolutely untenable position, since we live in a century in which there is no possible ideological detour around the concentration camp. *The Gulag Archipelago* finished Marxism as a spiritual force in the world. It did not end all Marxist regimes by any means, but it ended Marxism as a spiritual force. Morally it was now dead. The process that led to November 9, 1989, and the breaching of the Berlin Wall really began in 1973 with the publication of *The Gulag Archipelago*. With the possible exception of Sigmund Freud's *General Introduction to Psychoanalysis, The Gulag Archipelago* is the most influential book of the twentieth century. And unlike Freud, who had many highly educated followers who propagated his ideas, Solzhenitsyn worked in isolation, under constant threat of a return to prison.

He was expelled from the Soviet Union in 1974 and first visited the United States in 1975. What was the reaction in this country to the most famous writer in the world, winner of the Nobel Prize, a man who, like David, had slain a giant, a man who had altered the course of history? I would say that in the very highest levels of government and the very highest and most respected levels of intellectual life in the

United States, it was one of eye-averting embarrassment. The presence of this man was an enormous embarrassment to so many different people.

Think back to Gerald Ford, who happened to be President of the United States when Solzhenitsyn arrived. Solzhenitsyn was formally welcomed to the country at a dinner given by the AFL-CIO. The labor federation invited President Ford to attend that dinner. He declined, citing a longstanding dinner date with his daughter. This was a touching piece of paternal piety. We eventually learned that he was afraid of upsetting the delicate balance of détente (remember that word?), which had been achieved with one of Khrushchev's successors, that noted architect of peace, Leonid Brezhnev. Ford, Brezhnev, and Secretary of State Henry Kissinger found it a bit unsuitable to have the President of the United States welcome Aleksandr Solzhenitsyn.

What was the reaction of the *New York Times*? The coverage of Solzhenitsyn's appearance at that dinner and of his speech, his first speech in the United States after the tumultuous and highly publicized events of his expulsion from the Soviet Union, was buried as only the *Times* can bury an event. His second major address, which was in New York not long afterward, was covered only because of the perseverance of a single individual, Hilton Kramer, an employee of the *New York Times* at that point, a man with whom I have not agreed on every subject, but whose courage in this case I have to acknowledge. I believe it made the first page of the second section. The three major networks, the only three we had at that time, NBC, ABC, and CBS, all declined to show the television interview Solzhenitsyn had done in England before he arrived in the United States, an interview that had made headlines all over the world, including this country. It was finally shown by William Buckley on *Firing Line* on PBS.

Now, I cannot explain to you the attitude of the *Times* or of the major television networks, but I have a feeling that it had to do with the prevailing intellectual and literary climate in the United States at that time. People running television networks think of themselves as part of the intellectual world. True, they think of themselves as living in the slums of the intellectual world; nevertheless, they feel they are in it. They want to pull themselves up by their bootstraps. They do respond—as we learned during the war in Vietnam—very sensitively to the prevailing winds of the intellectual community. Which brings me specifically to that community and to the literary world and its reaction to Aleksandr Solzhenitsyn.

When Solzhenitsyn was introduced to the American public after his arrival here, who did the honors? Was there a blue-ribbon committee of major American writers who said, "Here is this giant whom we respect so much, whose works we have read so diligently"? No, he appeared on the arm of George Meany, president of the AFL-CIO. Was that because the AFL-CIO with its clout had muscled aside all the literary people who wanted to get closer to this man and had denied them the privilege of being host to Aleksandr Solzhenitsyn and welcoming him to the United States? Alas, that is not the case. Solzhenitsyn was perceived within the American literary community as a huge embarrassment, a violation of its etiquette. Etiquette is the key word.

For a start, he was a giant, and what literary world wants a giant to drop from the sky into its midst? I mean, it's an awkward and discomfiting sort of thing that upsets the existing rankings, the existing status order. But quite aside from that, one subtle and one not so subtle point must be made here. We were reminded over and over again, at the time of the great publicity about Solzhenitsyn's expulsion and at the time of his winning of the Nobel Prize, that here was a man who wrote in the tradition of Tolstoy, Turgenev, Lermontov, Saltykov, Gogol, and other giants of the Russian realistic tradition. Which is to say he wrote dramatic, emotionally charged stories presenting very full, very rich slices of contemporary life. The existence of a body of work such as this, awarded the Nobel Prize just five years before, was a reproach to what was going on in American fiction at that time — a trend that seemed unstoppable, that valued above all a prestigious anorexia, a sublime and deadpan withering away that is known as minimalism. It was very uncomfortable in a literary sense to have Solzhenitsyn's grand-scale realism suddenly represented by its author in the United States.

But that was not nearly as insufferable as the rudeness, the unforgivable rudeness, that Solzhenitsyn had expressed toward socialism and Marxism. Jean-François Revel, a French socialist who had run for the French Chamber of Deputies on the Socialist ticket, had kept hearing in the late 1960s about the imminent descent of the dark night of fascism in the United States. He heard this mainly from American writers, and he figured they must know what they were talking about. They were Americans, they were right here, they were observers. He came to this country to be on hand to record the cataclysm when it finally occurred. He toured the United States, returned to France, and wrote a book called *Neither Marx Nor Jesus*, in which he said, "In the United States I ran across one of the strangest phenomena in all of astronomy. The dark night of fascism is forever descending in America, but it only touches ground in Europe. This is a very odd sort of thing." He ascribed this obsession with fascism among literary people to what he called a "Marxist mist." He said there were very few Marxists in the United States, and I think he was absolutely correct about that. Nevertheless, he said, there was a misty notion of the inequalities of the class system out of which the fashionable ideas seemed to come. It had become a form of etiquette through which literary people established their aloofness from the mob, which today goes under the name of the middle class. I think he was absolutely correct about that, too.

In this country our literary people took this attitude: They said, "Obviously something went wrong in Hungary in 1956; and, really, the Soviets should not have invaded Czechoslovakia in 1968. There apparently were some forced-labor camps, but this was the fault of the madman Stalin who took socialism on a wrong turn. Mistakes happen." The unpardonable sin of Aleksandr Solzhenitsyn was to say, "No, these horrors were not due to Stalin. They were not due to Lenin, even though it was Lenin who invented not only the concentration camp — namely, a huge detention center in which you imprison not the enemy but your own people — but also the very term itself. Yet it was not even Lenin's fault. It cannot be blamed on communism as a political system. It lies at the door of a system of thought, Marxism. Any ideology that seeks a priori to recreate human morality from zero and gains power will lead to the same result."

In literary circles, particularly in New York literary circles, this was seen as a piece of very gauche effrontery. Just think, we had in this country no Bernard-Henri Levy, as France did, no André Glucksmann. These young thinkers, writers, philosophers on the left in France had been leaders of the fights on the barricades in 1968. But after reading *The Gulag Archipelago* they said, "We can no longer keep silent; communism, socialism, is a gigantic piece of moral degeneracy." Bernard-Henri Levy referred to it as "barbarism with a human face." Did that impulse ever reach our writers, artists, journalists, intellectuals on the left? Never. Or, rather, it never went beyond a tiny handful of mavericks such as David Horowitz. There was nothing remotely comparable to what went on in France, where intellectual consensus underwent a seismic shift.

So how did our intellectual community deal with

Solzhenitsyn? Through a whispering campaign.

Part of it was an aesthetic whispering campaign that went like this: This man was not given the Nobel Prize for literature, but for politics. I can't tell you how many writers told me, "You know, you can't read the man, he's basically unreadable." And I would say, "Really, you mean you couldn't read *One Day in the Life of Ivan Denisovich*? I can't imagine that you couldn't read it." "Well, I read it, but it's so shallow." They acted as if it was *Uncle Tom's Cabin*. So I said, "Tell me, what did you think of the character of Shukhov?" And they would say, "Well, I don't really remember him." In fact, in *One Day in the Life of Ivan Denisovich*, Shukhov is the name used in the text for Ivan Denisovich. The title itself is a piece of irony, because it is so polite to call this prisoner, Shukhov, by his first name and his patronymic, Ivan Denisovich. He's always Shukhov. The name is used constantly in that short novella. In fact, our writers could not bring their eyes to the pages for fear of being turned to pillars of salt, like Lot's wife, by the god of literary fashion. It was an extraordinary thing.

But most of the whispering campaign was political and, as always happens, psychological. "He's a Christian zealot." "He's an agrarian reactionary." (I don't know exactly where that came from. Solzhenitsyn was forced to live in the country when he went into permanent exile, but he has never struck me as very agrarian.) And on the psychological side: "He's an impossible man. He's one big spew of gall, bitterness, venom," and so on. And then with a hypocritical pity: "Well, you know, he suffered greatly in those camps. He's really not *right*, he's a little off."

In fact, this is a classic example of what Freud would have called resistance and denial. What was being denied? What was being denied was that our leading literary lights and our leading intellectuals generally had paid lip service for so long to what is perhaps the most pernicious ideology of the past two centuries and had averted their eyes and been apologists, long after the weight of evidence was in, for the most tyrannical regime of the twentieth century, one that finally outstripped, in its barbarity, even Hitler's Germany.

But I think that the breaching of the Berlin Wall has let loose a wind that will, in time, blow away the mist. I think that the resistance, the denial, will eventually come to an end. And I think intellectuals even in the United States, as they now do in Europe and throughout the world, will acknowledge the achievements, the extraordinary literary achievements, the great physical and moral courage, of Aleksandr Solzhenitsyn and the great battle for freedom that he has won.

The Marxists used to refer to the freight train of history, which they presumed ran on their track. And Stalin, only partly out of manipulative cunning, used to refer to writers as the engineers of the soul. Well, the freight train of history has finally arrived at its destination, and the engineer has turned out to be Aleksandr Solzhenitsyn.

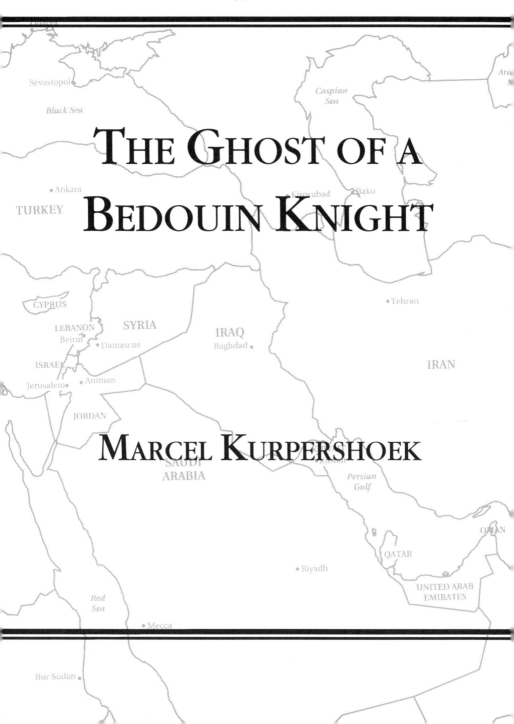

THE GHOST OF A BEDOUIN KNIGHT

MARCEL KURPERSHOEK

Marcel Kurpershoek was born in 1949 in The Hague, the Netherlands. He studied Arabic in Leyden and at Gizeh University in Cairo, Egypt. In 1975, he joined the Foreign Service in the Netherlands. He has served as a diplomat to Cairo, Damascus, Riyadh, The Hague, and at the United Nations. He is currently part of the Netherlands delegation to NATO in Brussels.

Dr. Kurpershoek is the author of *The Short Stories of Yusuf Idris* and *Diep in Arabië* (Deep Inside Arabia). His work has been published in several Dutch journals. He is a specialist in bedouin dialects and oral culture. He lived among the Utayba and Duwasir tribes in the Nejd, the inner Arabian desert, recording oral poetry and narratives, both modern and from the heroic age predating the establishment of the state of Saudi Arabia.

The results of Mr. Kurpershoek's fieldwork will be published in three volumes by E. J. Brill in Leyden. The first volume, entitled *The Poetry of Dindan, Bohemian of the Arabian Desert*, will appear in fall 1993. The following selection is an adaptation from his book *Diep in Arabië*.

T he Saudi capital of Riyadh, where I lived from 1986 until 1990, turned out to be a unique combination of Klondike boomtown, Baptist conference ground, and the Thousand and One Nights. Here were Japanese and Western businessmen in three-piece suits, zooming along superhighways through the city in air-conditioned taxis driven by Indian cabbies, on their way to a rendezvous with the Lebanese front man for a Saudi tycoon. Here was a *suq** where Yemenite shopkeepers yanked down their steel shutters five times a day at the first strains of the muezzin's call to rush to the mosques, goaded by their fear of the religious police of the Society for the Encouragement of Good and the Prevention of Evil. And here, too, were palatial neighborhoods where the lavender Rolls Royces, the fluorescent green, custom-made Mercedeses, the twin-axled Range Rovers, and the scarlet Lamborghinis of the Saudi upper class rolled through the ports of Hollywood castles surrounded by tropical gardens.

But where was the Arabia of Lawrence, of Charles Doughty, Wilfred Thesiger, St. John Philby, and all those other intrepid desert travelers? The Arabia of the bedouins and camels, of the black tents woven of goat-hair, of the cragged faces of desert foxes in a circle round the campfire, decorously passing each other little cups of bitter green coffee and telling stories in which the latest tribal wars are endlessly relived? And where was the Arabia that served as the cradle of Arabic poetry, poetry that reached its zenith fifteen hundred years ago in the desert scenes of the Mu'allaqat: the prize-winning odes legend tells us were hung on the door of the Ka'bah in pre-Islamic Mecca?

---

*suq — traditional Arab market held in arcaded alleyways.

In search of that Arabia, I inevitably wound up in the Nasim district of Riyadh, where bedouins from all over the country have settled and built homes, block by block, tribe by tribe. Here, amid copper coffeepots, in black tents set up in the back gardens of mansions, I met the country cousins who came to plead their cases before the capital-city bureaucracy, bedouins for whom the tent was a social meeting ground. Before long I noticed that my interest in their oral poetic tradition, a tradition that had kept alive the heroic past of their tribes, touched a sensitive, chauvinistic chord. This was how I established the contacts that I hoped would one day allow me to spread my network of informants out into the desert—away from the spotlights, the Ministry of Culture, and the doctors of Islamic law, out to the vast expanses where the old bedouin bravado still reigned supreme.

There is a street in an-Nasim named after one of the bedouins' most popular poets: Shleiwih al-Atauwi. The name means nothing to modern Saudi city dwellers. They are not interested in the old world of the bedouins, knowledge of which is administered either along with one's mother's milk, or not at all. But every bedouin knows that "al-Atauwi" means "a member of the group of Dhuwi Atia tribes belonging to the great Utayba confederation." And every bedouin knows that Shleiwih was a legendary desert knight of the last century who popped up everywhere in central Arabia to rob other tribes of their camels. The bedouins in an-Nasim were still able to expound with painstaking precision on Shleiwih's verses, one of which begins like this:

"I have given my heart to the speedy riding camels,
As though it was bound by cinches to the saddle.
Nothing can stop it, unless the wind should let itself be staid,
Or the foothills of the Begum tribe take off and run.

You who ask for me: know this, I am Shleiwih,
my heart determined to defy the dangerous course."

Later on in the poem, Shleiwih says: "When the weight
is trifling and my fellows are beside themselves, I leave
the weight to my fellows and take pride." A bedouin
knows immediately what Shleiwih means. When the
water supply ran out during a desert crossing, there was a
customary way to share the remainder among one's fel-
low-sufferers. The bedouins would take a drinking bowl,
place a stone in it, and fill the bowl until the water just
covered the stone, the "weight." Quarrels were prevented,
for everyone could see that the others received no more
than their fair share. Keeping the peace was no unneces-
sary precaution, for the men were truly "beside themselves," both with thirst and their desire for plunder.
Shleiwih, however, passed "the weight" along: He gave
up his ration of water. In this way, he proved that he could
be harder on himself than the others, that he was capable
of patiently bearing even the greatest deprivation. In
willpower, courage, stamina, and self-control, he stood
head and shoulders above his fellows. Demonstrating this
meant more to him than a last sip of water to ease his
parched throat.

Ironically enough, the next side street in an-Nasim is
named after Omar ibn Rubay'an, a name as irreconcilable
with that of Shleiwih as the positive poles of two bar mag-
nets. As scion of a family which, from father to son and
from time immemorial, has produced the sheiks of ar-
Ruga (one half of the Utyaba confederation; the other half
is called Barga), Omar embodied the pinnacle of his tribe's
aristocracy. The Rubay'ans' access to the court is guaranteed. Power, influence, and riches are a self-evident part of
their inheritance, and so they move through life with the
ease, natural grace, and calm dignity (sometimes misinter-
preted as modesty) that mark true nobility.

Shleiwih, on the other hand, was a classic example of the "upstart," a man driven to find his place in the sun, to right the wrong of his lowly birth and break through the social layers above him at any cost. Shleiwih excelled in the two arts held in greatest esteem by the bedouins: the raiding of enemy tribes and the art of poetry. Transferred to America, his might have been a rags-to-riches story. But in the conservative world of the desert, energy and talent are not enough to extract one from the social flypaper of one's own class. In the eyes of the Rubay'ans he remained, despite his fame, a piffling troublemaker with the pretensions of a parvenu.

As befits a knight, Shleiwih died in harness. The poems and stories in which he played the leading role more than a century ago have spread out over hundreds of miles, to all the tribes that once lay within the swathe of his pillaging. And today, both friend and foe see him as the quintessence of the bedouin ideal: the great hunter, trotting eternally across the desert on his camel, insatiable in his thirst for glory. In this way the Shleiwih cycle has become part of the great, unwritten desert romance of chivalry; the *chansons de geste** with which the tribes keep alive the memory of the heroic and independent past, and by which they resist the great democratic effacement that threatens their identity.

Fascinated by the stories of my Utaybi friends in an-Nasim, I set off for Afif, three hundred miles west of Riyadh, to conduct an investigation into the oral legacy of the robber baron Shleiwih. In my pocket I carried the combination so indispensable to opening the safe of local bedouin memory: a letter of recommendation signed by the deputy governor of Riyadh province. Experience had taught me that it was only after one had displayed a

---

chansons de geste—epic poems of the French Middle Ages based on historical or legendary persons or events.

certificate of this sort that the bedouins felt safe enough to open their oral troves.

So I arrived one afternoon at the home of Ibn Shleiwih, "the son of Shleiwih," as the bedouins call the great-grandson Khalid. Seen from across the vast plain, the housing complex was nothing more than a pair of pebbles on both sides of the dark, narrow ribbon that marked the old road from Mecca to Riyadh. I left the paved road and drove through the dust to the port of the weathered one-story building. After some extensive banging on the trellises, the port was opened by a sleepy-looking Asian servant. He led me across the graveled courtyard to the house and ushered me into the reception room, a low, dark, rectangular space without a trace of furniture. There were worn carpets on the ground, and pillows and arm-rests against the wall.

After a while the gentleman of the house arrived, wearing the traditional white robe and a red-and-white checkered headdress held firmly in place by black bands. He invited me to be seated on the other side of a red-leather camel saddle. Khalid ibn Shleiwih was short and rather sturdy, with something sullen about his eyes and mouth and with a pitch-black goatee that protruded stubbornly from his chin. When he spoke, he spoke succinctly, his gestures were formal. He emitted no *joie de vivre*, no bubbling spirit, but a sober forcefulness, as though he harbored many bitter thoughts but was too proud to speak them aloud.

He asked me brusquely what had brought me to Afif, and how I had come to call on him. I said I was looking for the descendants of Shleiwih, with the firm intention of using only reliable information from authoritative sources. That was why the bedouins had sent me to him. Khalid relaxed and smiled approvingly. That was correct; if I was interested in the legacy of Shleiwih I had come to the right place.

After I had passed this rather abrupt examination, the ice was broken. I handed him the letter from the deputy governor of Riyadh. Khalid held the page up to the light for a while with the air of an examining civil servant, but finally called in his eldest son, a high school student, and said gruffly: "Read what it says!" The boy meekly did as he was ordered, and Khalid nodded. He was prepared to tell all he knew. But in view of the wealth of material stored in his memory, it would be better if I stayed with him and settled in at his plantation just across the road to Mecca.

For four weeks I was a part of the household. In the evenings we would go to tribal meetings, where Khalid recited the poems of his great-grandfather and told stories of Shleiwih's illustrious feats of arms. During the day he would receive bedouins in the portico of the front courtyard, or he would be off maintaining his contacts and practicing tribal politics. In word and gesture he meticulously cultivated the ideal image of the sheik dished up for the bedouins in the poems and stories of their forefathers.

One morning I found him seated in the portico, in the company of a wildly gesturing tribesman. The visitor was screaming that he would kill so-and-so, slit his throat, in other words do something drastic if Khalid did not help him undo the injustice he had suffered. The supplicant occasionally kissed his own hand and then stroked it lightly over Khalid's beard, all the while invoking the name of Shleiwih and the other forefathers. Khalid listened in silence, to all appearances unmoved. Finally he broke off the visitor's flood of words with the brusque announcement that he would take up the matter at the town hall in Afif after Friday, the Muslim day of rest. Later Khalid told me that a sheik commands respect by virtue of his *simt*, his dignified silence. *Simt* is seen as a sign of intelligence and insight into affairs of the world. When matters of importance are discussed in the *majlis,* the circle of men on the carpet, the sheik, whose responsibility it is to pilot his tribe through uncertainty and danger, shows himself to be a man of few words. He listens, resting on one elbow on the cushion, his fingers toying thoughtfully with his prayer beads. Then everyone knows that the sheik is busy "braiding and twisting," in other words, he is in the process of twisting and tying a mental rope. On the basis of accurate insight he arrives at an unshakable decision. The sheiks are "men like mountains anchored in the earth," bulwarks of indomitability and strength in the company of common people.

A sheik who wishes to carry weight in higher circles cannot do without status. Camels have always been a traditional part of one's status; these days, a plantation is indispensable as well. Yet Khalid's agricultural project was not exactly an economic success. The area around Afif is ideal pastureland for the bedouin herds. The saline plants, which camels love and which give their milk its flavor and rich nutritional content, thrive here. But the salty groundwater does not lend itself to farming. Every few days Faqiallah, Khalid's Pakistani hired man with whom I shared the shed on the plantation, scooped handfuls of salt from the motor of the irrigation pump.

When the irrigation channels dried up, the water left a white film behind. The palm trees remained gaunt and struggled to survive. The fields of clover yielded less with each passing year. What was growing now was no more than a clump here and there on the salt-glazed earth. Faqiallah didn't kid himself. He had told Khalid often enough that the plantation was a lost cause, no matter how hard he worked. But Khalid wouldn't dream of giving up. The princes and dignitaries in Riyadh were, without exception, gentlemen farmers in their free time. These days, a green pleasure garden amid the dunes was every bit as fitting as falconry, Arabian thoroughbreds, purebred camels, and other attributes of power and true Arabism.

Khalid's dignity and his ambitions as sheik demanded that he maintain a farm as prestige object, no matter what the financial consequences. If nature wasn't going to help out, then that was nature's tough luck.

Khalid has never been a bedouin, not in the sense of one who leads a nomadic existence with his herds. The house he lives in was built by his father, Mash'an, who also left him the camels. Khalid doesn't need the animals for his livelihood. Like the plantation, they are a status symbol. Each is pedigreed, and their color—one half of the herd is black, the other white—ups their prestige value even further. Khalid himself has little to do with these animals. It's enough that they are there: a living reminder of the heroic deeds of his forefathers who rustled the herd together, and proof that Khalid has not abandoned his roots in the bedouin world.

The female dromedaries are herded into the desert each morning. There they graze on the tussocks of dried grass, under the watchful eye of a Sudanese servant who thumps and bangs around behind the animals in a dilapidated Nissan Hilux. Toward evening they return home on their own, in a long file headed by their prima donna, to spend the night in the enclosure behind the house. During the mating season, which begins halfway through the fall, the males stay in their separate pens: one for the black male, the other for Khalid's pride and joy, the white stud Alyan, a present from a prince of the house of Saud. Visitors are shown the royal brand on Alyan's haunch. Khalid's own brand can be found on the camel's long neck; the two vertical stripes of the Dhuwi Atia are somewhat comparable to the state colors and mottoes of a license plate. The individual owner, however, can be traced by the license number itself, the "witness." In Khalid's case, the witness is a figure in the shape of a staff with a curved grip, burned into the hair of the animal's neck between the vertical stripes of the Dhuwi Atia.

Like his entire identity and position in society, Khalid inherited this "witness" from his great-grandfather, Shleiwih. Shleiwih in turn received his brand as a tribute from an opponent he had robbed. One evening, during a visit to his father-in-law, Khalid told me the whole story.

During one of his first raids, Shleiwih stole a herd of camels from the Qahtan, the traditional enemies of the Utayba. "He divided the black camels among the members of his party," Khalid said. "As leader of the raid, he kept the white ones himself. That was the custom. Exactly one year later he set up camp in a *wadi** northwest of Afif. At the end of the day, after late afternoon prayers, a rider on a fast camel came racing up. The rider had his animal kneel at the entrance to Shleiwih's tent. Shleiwih received the traveler with open arms, fed him, and let him spend the night in his tent. Shleiwih did not ask why he had come or who he was—he asked no questions at all.

"The next morning the man said: 'Shleiwih, you have received me honorably. You have gone to great lengths to make me comfortable, and you have not asked me a single question about myself.'

"Shleiwih answered, 'May God grant you long life, you are welcome to stay as long or as briefly as it pleases you.'

"'I am Ghazi al-Midla,' the man said, 'of Qahtan, the owner of the white camels there at the well.'

"'You are welcome, al-Midla, from the first moment of your visit to the last. Do not worry, your wish will be fulfilled: Rise, go to where the camels are lying and take them all!'

"'No,' al-Midla said, 'I have not come to retrieve my camels, son of Ma'iz. You have taken them fair and square, as is the custom between our tribes. Sometimes we are robbed, the next time it's your turn. No, I have not come for my camels, I have come to make a very humble

---

wadi—valley, or stream that is dry except during periods of rainfall.

81

request.'

"'Speak and it is yours,' was the reply.

"'It's about the staff, the brand on their neck. Please do not remove it, but take it as your own mark for all time.'

"'Your wish is granted,' Shleiwih said.

"Ever since that day, this has remained the brand of Shleiwih, the same brand I now use on my camels. He never again used his old brand, the brand of his father Ma'iz."

Khalid was in good form that evening. The night was of velvet, his listeners well-disposed from the start. Freed for a few hours from the cares that accompanied his position as tribal leader, and the bitter thought of the intrigues being hatched by his enemies, Khalid warmed his heart before the glorious past. A smoking pot of fragrant sandalwood was brought out to put both speaker and listeners in the proper mood.

After these preparations had been made, Khalid was ready to relate again what he had heard from his father, Mash'an, who had heard it in turn from grandfather Fajir. The story told of how great-grandfather Shleiwih had fought free of his lowly origins and won a place in the bedouin aristocracy "by virtue of his strong arm." Shleiwih's father, Ma'iz, belonged to the desert rank and file. His fellow tribesmen referred to him disrespectfully as "Bobah," meaning "one who scrapes his backside clean in the sand after a bowel movement." But fate had other things in store for his energetic son. Even as a boy, Shleiwih was goaded by a restless spirit. During one of his solitary wanderings he happened upon a man and a woman, deep in sleep beside their camels. He stabbed the man, a black slave, to death with the man's own dagger. The woman, awake now and fearful, he allowed to return on her own camel to her father, al-Harf of the Harb tribe.

After this promising start, Shleiwih decided he was cut out for a career as a self-employed bandit. He would no longer settle for a mere share of the loot as a follower of the Rubay'ans, the upper sheiks of the Ruga. No, he gave up his steady job and went free-lance. Like all young entrepreneurs, his first problem was to draw customers away from the established competition. And, like each successive generation of rebels pounding at the gates of authority, he was frustrated in his efforts by the deep-rooted conservatism of the human animal. When Shleiwih announced his plans one spring, at the start of the rustling season, his tribesmen laughed in his face and left him standing alone next to the camel he had stolen from the Harb. No one even dreamed of giving up the excellent chances for loot they would have as followers of the Rubay'ans for the uncertain prospects of the young hero. Embittered, Shleiwih then put fresh heart into his camel with the following poem:

"I'll run you ragged, little camel of Harf, so help me;
As sure as I'm standing here, I speak without jesting.
I found no comrade to walk with you side by side;
All said: 'The gray masses we will follow.'
A splendid animal, swaying her hips through the dry valley,
Like a woman who has left her husband and in her father's tent hankers for a real man.
Verily, you shall hear the herders with your own ears,
Hooting to round up their white purebreds.
Then you will have my cloak for company in the dark
As I, despite the barking dogs, move in on my prey."

When he returned from the raid, driving his booty before him, people began to take notice. Shleiwih had proven his professional competence. But now fate came to test his moral fiber. He had no trouble finding volunteers for the following foray. The problem, however, was that a certain Da'ul, a sad sack and notorious jinx, had also signed up for the raid. Shleiwih's partners presented him with an ultimatum: Either Da'ul stayed home, or they would. But Shleiwih declared that he held no truck with *shirk*, the belief in a force other than the one God. And although three quarters of his soldiery stuck to their refusal to ride with Da'ul, this was the raid during which Shleiwih made off with al-Midla's herd of black and white camels. Divvying up the loot upon his return, Shleiwih said: "Here you go, Da'ul, these sixteen camels are for you. Now you should be able to feed your children." Then he turned to the dumbfounded stay-at-homes and spoke this verse:

"Nest of heretics, the Lord has not forgotten Da'ul:
God grants a living to those he sees fit."

Shleiwih's reputation as a robber chieftain was established. The new star in the bandits' firmament had demonstrated his independence. His courage and his mastery of the art of the raid, his unshakable belief in himself and in God's merciful kindness, his eye for the needs of his followers, all these things were beyond dispute. Like Robin Hood, he used his thieving arts to promote social justice in the desert. The only thing needed to complete the image of a gallant knight was the admiration of his Dulcinea.

This void was filled during the third and final raid of the cycle. During this foray, Shleiwih had thrust his way into the furthest corner of Qahtan tribal territory, almost to the border between the Qahtan and the Duwasir. He left his companions to rest while he climbed a granite peak to survey the surroundings. Once at the top, he saw that the plain on the other side was dotted with the bumpy silhouettes of camels. At that same moment, however, he heard a girl's voice singing. Shleiwih crept out onto the overhang under which the girl was sitting, and listened:

"The youth with the sword has hounded me
Like a herd of camels headed up by Shleiwih,
White she-camels stolen from the land of Qahtan,
Bounty for the one whipping on his speedy mount,
He eyed his prey from the high mountain,
From the summit of Saradih he swooped down.
Singing he disappeared beyond the horizon,
Too far to worry about any dawn attacks.
My love has pressed his branding iron to my heart
    strings,
Again and again, until my knees gave way."

Shleiwih realized that the girl had heard of his raid on
the camels of al-Midla, and that she had made him the
knight of her dreams. Moved, he came out of hiding and
introduced himself as the hero of her song. As a token of
gratitude, he allowed the girl to take her own animals to
safety before he and his men attacked and took off with
the rest of the tribe's property. The girl remained so faith-
ful to her romantic idol that she refused to let her fellow
herders use her camels to go and warn the owners.

It was only as evening fell the next day, when the bandits had disappeared beyond reach, that she returned to
camp and faced her father's rage for Shleiwih's sake.
"Cursed be the furrows in which you were sown," the
father shouted in the dialect of the Qahtan. "Why didn't
you sound the alarm when our camels were stolen?"
"How could I," the girl replied, "when Shleiwih had made
me a present of my own camels? How could I put Qahtan
on the heels of one who treated me so courteously?"

Shleiwih had the misfortune of living at a time when the
Middle Ages were coming to an end in Arabia. Shleiwih
al-Atauwi was still in time to use his "strong arm" to work
his way up to the status of formidable bandit leader, and

so become sheik of the Mehadla tribe of the Dhuwi Atia confederation. His descendants, however, would be stopped in their tracks. During their lifetimes, King Abdul Aziz (better known in the West as Ibn Saud) established the state's monopoly on violence, banned the bedouins' raids on neighboring tribes, and generously rewarded good behavior. The new order benefited the presiding elite and checked the mobility of energetic upstarts. This was not only convenient for the Rubay'ans, the sheiks of all Ruga (including Dhuwi Atia), but also for the conservative tribal leaders in the lower echelons. All their interests were served by preventing those such as Shleiwih from leapfrogging over the sheiks of the Ghananim and other subtribes to demand precedence among the Atauwis, from establishing their primacy over the entire Dhuwi Atia group. For even today, due partly to the fact that a century in the desert is as a decade to our own sense of time, no one has forgotten Shleiwih's lowly origins. For great-grandson Khalid, therefore, only one of the two paths taken by Shleiwih remained open: that of poetry in the service of his own political ambition.

One day I was driving through the desert with Mnif, sheik of the Ghananim. We were on our way to visit bedouins who still lived in tents among their camels, horses, and greyhounds. Mnif had great news. "The fifth one has risen," he announced cheerfully. The fifth star of the seven comprising the Big Bear had been seen above the horizon. This meant that in twenty-five days the *wasmi* would arrive, the ascendancy of the stars Canopus, the Pleiades, and Gemini: Arabian fall.

If it rained heavily during this period, particularly during the rise of the Pleiades, the desert grass and annuals would reach full bloom and the camels would be able to graze to their content even before winter began. Mnif said the bedouins were poised between hope and fear. Not a drop of rain had fallen during three consecutive *wasmis*, and the dearth of edible plants and grasses had driven bedouins out of the desert in growing numbers. When the animals must be fed with supplies bought and brought in from outside, the charm of nomadic life quickly wears thin. The die-hards we were going to visit had to bring in seven sacks of barley each day to feed their seventy camels: an outlay of almost a thousand dollars a month.

On the way out, Mnif explained the workings of the Ruga branch of the Utayba confederation. He brushed off Khalid's claim to the sheikdom of all Dhuwi Atia tribes as "absolute nonsense." Khalid was emir of the Abla settlement, in other words, of his own property and the house and land of one other Saudi family, and the sheik of his own subtribe, the Mehadla: nothing more.

"He'd better watch his step," Mnif said as his Landcruiser roared through the deep ruts in the sand. "The Ministry of Information will never let him call himself the sheik of Dhuwi Atia, not in a book; besides that, all his swaggering might just get him thrown in the slammer."

"Look." He produced an identity card from the breast pocket of his robe. "It says here that I am the emir of the Ghananim in Afif and surroundings. And that," he said, tapping his finger on the plastic, "is the seal of Riyadh province. Khalid has no authority over us."

"But he tells wonderful stories," I protested, "that's all I'm interested in; not in figuring out who's the boss of the Dhuwi Atia."

Mnif was willing to admit that Khalid was a skillful raconteur. But he "embellished" the stories about his forefathers: He blew them up and added all kinds of things, as long as they suited his purposes. The poems were the only things I could I could rely on, Mnif warned, for they were immovably fixed in meter and rhyme. If Khalid were to tamper with the poems, it would be noticed immediately. Mnif meant that the collective memory of the tribe served as a fail-safe against abuse of their poetic heritage, in much the same way the KGB once guarded the coded keys to Moscow's doomsday arsenal. Like pits in the dates, the poems were hard kernels of truth within the perishable fruit of the stories.

I began to realize that I could burn my fingers quite badly if my poetic research should happen to fan the smoldering fire of this struggle for precedence between sheiks. Afif was a china shop through which I had to step carefully, on stocking feet. For my own good I would have to don the guise of political birdbrain and cling to the fiction that my verses had nothing to do with present-day reality. I was simply gamboling about, in pursuit of my exotic butterflies.

Officially, the sheiks, the tribal chieftains, are the same as any other Saudi. When King Abdul Aziz finally obtained the monopoly on political power, his leadership was recognized by the rest of the world. The traditional tribal pasturelands fell into the hands of the state and were then redistributed. Of course, the land was usually awarded to the same tribal leaders who had always ruled over it, but the state reserved the right to withdraw this favor if the sheiks did not march to the tune of the newly established order. The bedouin raids on the possessions of others were now regarded as common criminality, not as the gallant sport and supreme expression of their sovereign freedom.

In theory, all Saudis were now equal before the law, just as they had always been equal in the sight of God. The Koran had been proclaimed the constitution, while the common laws were based on the *shari'a,* the Islamic law. The new authorities could therefore insist that they were doing nothing more than rectifying a heathen abuse in order to return to the form of government Allah had ordained by the word of his Prophet.

Generally speaking, the sheiks had no trouble resigning themselves to this less exalted role. Mnif, for example, voiced the official viewpoint without a trace of hard feelings. The emir of the tribe is there to settle the differences between bedouins out of court, to testify to the records officer that a certain person is in fact a member of his tribe and therefore eligible for Saudi identification papers, or to vouch for a tribesman who has been taken into custody and thereby make him eligible for bail. The emir, in other words, serves as intermediary between the government and the common bedouin and therefore saves the authorities a great deal of work.

Yet Khalid was a case apart. His whole being revolted against the self-effacing notion that the role of the sheik was that of a kind of social worker on behalf of the state. The fact that Mnif did hold to this notion was for Khalid only further proof that his rival was nothing more than what he scornfully referred to as a *mu'arrif,* a character witness for his fellow tribesmen.

"He's not a real sheik," Khalid said, "he didn't inherit the tribal leadership from his father the way I did. The Ghananim of Afif held a meeting one day and chose him as their representative." In other words, Mnif was nothing more than a parvenu, one who had allowed himself to be elected democratically and was therefore obligated, if he hoped to hold on to his title, to perform services for his constituency. "Mnif is all right," Khalid was ready to admit, "but he shouldn't go around pretending to be more than he really is."

It seemed to me not entirely in my own interests to remind Khalid that he, in turn, owed his status to the son of an underdog, to a man who had worked his way up to the status of robber baron by virtue of his "strong arm" and who had become sheik because other riffraff, by "voting with their feet" (and, therefore, more or less democratically), had elected him to that position. Khalid would surely have retorted that Shleiwih had not built his career on amicability and helpfulness, but on proving himself the toughest cameleer and the best fighter. Shleiwih was not the product of hypocritical slave morality; he was the alpha male of the troop.

Khalid touted his complete lack of patience with fawning and democratic toadyism by his display of *kheshuna*, bedouin bluntness, by his terse, brusque manner of expression. This was also the style in which he fought out his private feuds: ruthlessly, openly, uncompromisingly. In the eyes of a well-adapted sheik such as Mnif, this was one of Khalid's bad traits. Of course, everyone had colleagues they didn't like, but that was no reason to rock the boat and submit opponents to a merciless social boycott the way Khalid did.

Had Khalid lived a century before, during the time of his famous great-grandfather, he could have fought out his differences with the spear and the sword. By means of diplomacy and violence, the two instruments of political ambition that the Prophet had known to manipulate with such mastery, he could have bound the tribes to himself and imposed his supreme authority on all of the Dhuwi Atia. The amiable Mnif, who rocked along so jollily behind his fat belly, would surely have been in the palm of his hand. These days the envy is kept on the boil, but there is no way to blow off steam. No one wishes to collide with the all-mighty state, and the sheiks are kept on a short leash. And so the feuds fester on in the form of jealousy, backbiting, and whispering campaigns.

Khalid wasn't intimidated by this. The thick, elongated notebook in which I copied his stories as neatly as possible in Arabic from my scribbled notes was, to his mind, the chronicle and testament of his knightly ancestry. He himself pointed to the place where he wished to see his name written, right at the top of the blank page on the inside cover. I wrote: "This book was transcribed from the mouth of Khalid ibn Mash'an ibn Fajir ibn Shleiwih, Emir of Abla and Emir of the tribe of Dhuwi Atia, now head of the sheikdom of Shleiwih al-Atauwi."

Like a politician on the campaign trail, Khalid is on the road every evening in his bid for recognition. Tonight he has been asked to add luster to a gathering of the Ghananim—in the absence, of course, of Mnif, the sheik of this subtribe of Dhuwi Atia. At a gas station just before Afif, Khalid swings his four-wheel-drive left, into the desert. At first the bouncing headlights shine only on a stretch of bare earth, but a little later the red taillights of a car show up in the distance as our beacon. Nine or ten bedouin vehicles—pickup trucks and Toyota Landcruisers—are parked up ahead. The Ghananim are seated in a semicircle on the ground, around a charcoal fire above which they are roasting a sheep. We park our sandals in the long line of bedouin footwear at the edge of the carpet and Khalid assumes his appointed place, at the head of the *majlis*, leaning on a cushion. As his personal chronicler, I am allowed to sit at his left hand. In the middle of the circle of men stands, as always, the boy with the coffeepot. He holds a stack of little porcelain cups without handles, only a few sizes bigger than thimbles, balanced on the palm of his right hand. From the long spout of the pot in his other hand he pours a thin stream of coffee into whichever cup is at the top of the stack—"like a silken thread," as the poet says.

Above us, the night desert sky is glittering. To the east the Pleiades are risen, sparkling like a tiara. Lower, just above the horizon, Aldebaran, the red star of Taurus, comes into view, "throbbing like the heart of a wolf," as the red stars are described in the old poems of the seasons. The simile is perfect; stars high on the heavens radiate a cold and constant light, but when they have just risen above the horizon they flicker and blink as though sending out signals.

Khalid's repertoire is familiar to all, but apparently never grows old. No one seems to tire of hearing how Shleiwih outfoxed other tribes and made mincemeat of them. Half the men present have their own two cents to add to the history of the tribe. Only one religious zealot, his headdress arranged in a staunch, crisp fold, pinched at the front and without the doubled-up headband of the bedouins, misses the point by reciting a poem full of homely wisdom and devout profundities.

In these circles talk does not deal with international politics, financial affairs, or stock market reports; the collapse of Communist regimes in Eastern Europe even as they speak causes no ripple in these men's desert sand. Talk here is of the tribe, its history, and the significance of that history for the genealogical classification of the bedouins.

"Have you already become an Utaybi?"

"Of course," I reply, "but then a Rugi, not a Bargauwi." I belong to their half of the Utayba tribe, but not to the other.

The cheering is unanimous, a success as cheaply won as Kennedy's at the Berlin Wall when he shouted, "*Ich bin ein Berliner,*" but that is the order one follows here: First you are a member of the Ghananim, then a member of Dhuwi Atia, then of the Ruga, then the Utyaba, and then finally, surrounding all this, comes a thin shell of Saudi identity. And so the men sit contentedly on their carpet beneath the starry desert sky, recalling events of more than a century ago as though they had happened yesterday, and as though they knew the main chracters personally.

"Look," Khalid says, "Shleiwih lived the way he described it in this poem:

"'God be praised, I've never been a ladies' man,
It must have been my nature, or else my self-control.
For aye we ride our camels thin with use
And drink from wells where only jackals howl.
Impatiently we take our riding crops and prod the
    dough upon the fire;
The sun has set but we still ride for hours.

At night we have our gnashing mounts kneel down,
Not far from tents spread out in broad array;
I walk to them, as though I were an honored guest,
When the sweet-lipped one is sleeping, beside the
    thrown-off veil,
I pat the watchdog, then slip through tent ropes without
    a sound,
To steal the she-camel the stud loves best.'

"That's how Shleiwih was," Khalid says proudly,
"unflinching, always on the prowl, the best camel rustler
of his day. Love, women, everything that was tender, fine,
and soft, he avoided it all like the plague. He spurned love
poetry, except for that one time when he said:

"'For my love I'd give everything on legs,
The bedouins and the veiléd womenfolk;
For her I'd give Ibn Rashid of Shammar,
Who brings the bedouin tribes to rack and ruin,
For her I'll even give my horses,
Our sheep and camels with their vaulted chests.
Oh, the sheik will forgive me, even unto eighty
    blunders
And what the other dimwits say, that leaves me cold.'

"When these verses came to the attention of Muhammad
Abdallah ibn Rashid, the ruler of Hail, his courtiers said:
'How can Shleiwih al-Atauwi ransom a powerful ruler
such as your highness for a woman?'

"But the sheik answered: 'As surely as I am the brother
of Nura, Shleiwih has made only one blunder, and he has
asked me to overlook eighty. What's more, I'm no dimwit.'
Then Ibn Rashid composed the following verse:

"'Bear this, my message, to Shleiwih
To purify me of all blame:

The sheik I am as yet, there is no knot I cannot cut;
In the height of summer I run my racing camels raw.
God help me, I know why he'd trade me for his beloved,
For I too have been through much for love:
The ladies always wrapped me around their little fin-
gers,
Tightly, like threads pulled taut between the needles.'"

The bedouins listen, breathless: Shleiwih, the stable-
man's son, dueling in verse on an equal footing with the
most powerful man in the Arabia of that day! They are
completely under the storyteller's spell: The voice they
hear is not that of Khalid, but of Ibn Shleiwih, great-grandson of the sheik of Dhuwi Atia; through him, the great
robber baron himself speaks to the Ghananim.

Just as Faulkner in his novels evoked the spirit of his legendary great-grandfather — the Old Colonel, who fought in
the Civil War and worked his way up from hillbilly to rail-
road baron — so Khalid takes on the form of Shleiwih.
From his mouth come the verses, the hard pits in the dates
of the stories, which his great-grandfather was the first to
speak.

And somewhere tonight, on the moonlit prairies of the
bedouin Valhalla, Shleiwih is out on yet another raid, riding with unflagging energy, forever sheik of the Ghananim
and all the other tribes of Dhuwi Atia.

Translated from the Dutch by Sam Garrett

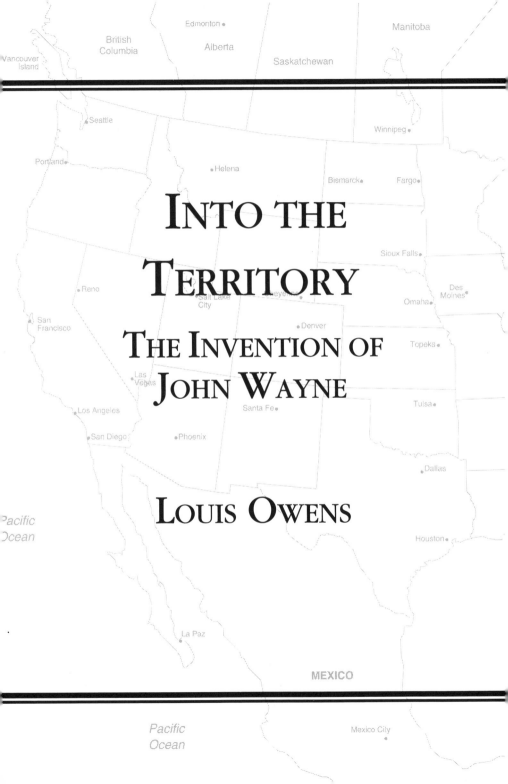

INTO THE
TERRITORY
THE INVENTION OF
JOHN WAYNE

LOUIS OWENS

Louis Owens was born in Lompoc, California in 1948. He spent eight years, seasonally, with the U.S. Forest Service, primarily as a wilderness ranger and firefighter. He received a Ph.D. in English from the University of California, Davis.

Dr. Owens, who is part Choctaw and part Cherokee, was awarded the PEN Josephine Miles Award for multicultural writing in 1993 for his books *Other Destinies: Understanding the American Indian Novel* and *The Sharpest Sight*. He received a National Endowment for the Arts creative writing award in 1988-89, and a National Endowment for the Humanities award to support work on Native American fiction in 1987. Dr. Owens taught for a year in Pisa, Italy, in 1980 under a Fulbright Fellowship.

He is also the author of the novel *Wolfsong* as well as of a number of critical studies. His writing has appeared in numerous publications including *North American Review*, the *Los Angeles Times*, and *American Indian Quarterly*.

Dr. Owens is a professor of literature and creative writing at the University of California, Santa Cruz. He is currently working on a novel, *Bone Game*. He lives in Boulder Creek, California, with his wife, Polly; daughters Elizabeth and Alexandra; and dog, Chama.

I grew up distrusting John Wayne. Even before I learned that the "Duke" began as a Midwestern boy named Marion Michael Morrison, I suspected that he wasn't real. For one thing, he seemed too big and too inescapable, always there during my childhood, spurring his horse across all of our lives. For another thing, I was conscious of being Indian — part Choctaw on my father's side and part Cherokee on my mother's. And Indians inhabited a troubled space in John Wayne movies. It wasn't that Indians — fullbloods like Geronimo or mixedbloods like me — were simply moving targets in his films, as they were in most Westerns of my childhood. In John Wayne movies Indians were treated somewhat decently, with at least a passing nod to their humanity. But there was an ever-present sense that the Indian didn't really count and was just a colorful remnant of the past, with no real stake in the world John Wayne was helping to construct. In the evenings in my grandparents' house (a big converted barn), I would watch my mixedblood Choctaw grandmother let her hair down, so long it almost touched the floor, and brush it with slow, thoughtful strokes, and I would wonder where she might fit into John Wayne's world. I suspected that she would be one of the obstacles John Wayne would have to eliminate. I'd listen to my mother talk about Cherokee country back in Oklahoma, what she still referred to as the "Nation," and try without success to connect this world of family stories and rich mixedblood Indian history with the empty place called the "Territory" in the Westerns. It was obvious to me that John Wayne didn't know the whole story.

As a ten-year-old, I listened to young Breck Coleman — John Wayne's role in "The Big Trail," a 1930 film ancient even in my childhood — explain, "You see, the Indians was my friends. They taught me all I know about the woods. They taught me how to follow a trail...And they taught me how to make the best bow and arrows too." Even to my ten-year-old ears, the words rang false. If the young white man had stopped short of the last line, I might have bought the whole thing; but I didn't believe Indians would ever have taught that guy how to make "the best bow and arrows, too." They wouldn't have trusted a guy who talked like that. I thought he was making it up, the way a kid would, and the silly voice sounded too much like Bobby Huff's, the white kid I played with at the other end of our three-mile gravel road. When I found out John Wayne's real name was Marion, I knew I was right. He'd made up everything.

The truth about John Wayne is that he was indeed the great American cowboy hero, throwing his stalking shadow across the continent and beyond. And he did, in fact, make everything up, reinventing himself during an incredible career in the same way that America has for five hundred years invented itself out of its fevered imagination. In the course of more than 150 films, Marion Morrison grew into the giant figure America demanded, molding himself to match the nation's psychic craving for an archetypal hero fitted to the great myth of the American West. When he died in 1979, the whole world knew clearly that a hero was gone. The essential truth about the great American hero, however, is its falseness. And that falseness is illuminated brilliantly in the shape-shifting that allowed a young Iowan named Marion Morrison to journey into the mythical American West and become something grand and new and strangely pure.

The West the "Duke" rode through was, and continues to be, the greatest dream of all. It is the place where we slough off our old names and old histories, shed whatever flaws we bear, and make ourselves anew. This phenomenal process began, of course, with the Pilgrims and

Puritans who looked westward from the Atlantic shore and saw the Promised Land of something they called the New World. In this untainted New World the European could begin again, unencumbered by anything as old as yesterday. And if the Old World threatened to catch up with him, he could continue westward, ahead of history. He could re-imagine himself, leave Marion Morrison behind and become John Wayne, the Duke. In the West, no one asked questions.

The true hero of the American West is beyond mundane law because he is beyond its reach—beyond civilization—and he operates not within the laws of man but within those of God. His great novel *Huckleberry Finn*, Mark Twain once explained, was about a struggle between "a sound heart and a deformed conscience," a struggle the heart wins. At the end of the novel, however, Huck knows he can live true to his heart only by escaping from civilization. He declares his intent to "light out for the Territory ahead of the rest." The "Territory," which ultimately became the state of Oklahoma (a name derived from the Choctaw language) is Indian Territory, that area set aside by the federal government to contain tribes forcibly removed from the East, their traditional homelands stolen by whites. My mother's ancestors, the Cherokee Nation, had walked from Georgia and North Carolina all the way to the Territory, 4,000 of them dying along the way from disease, starvation, and brutality on what the people call the "Trail of Tears." Most of my father's tribe, the Choctaw, had also gone to the Territory. To many Indians, the Territory was a new home, a safe place for families shattered by the Removal. For white Americans, however, Indian Territory—anything west of the Missouri—became a fantastic realm beyond civilized consciousness and conscience. In an important sense, the entire American West was "Indian Territory," where men (seldom women) lived according to the heart, not the social conscience.

To live true to the "sound heart" — and to impose the rules of that heart on a lawless place — requires that the hero approach, in all innocence, a state of divinity. Such a man was Natty Bumppo, the Deerslayer, of James Fenimore Cooper's nineteenth-century romance novels, and such a man was John Wayne, the direct descendant of Natty. Natty himself, of course, was descended from Lancelot of the Arthurian romances, the flower of knight errantry in fruitless quest of the Holy Grail. For the American cowboy-quester, the grail is the American dream of endless youth and unlimited potential, free of the constraints of civilization that puts the values of family and community first. That so many Western heroes are called "Kid" — Billy the Kid, the Comanche Kid, the Ringo Kid — testifies to America's desire to hold to a self-willed innocence associated with a pre-adult state. Roaming the West without families to constrain their behavior — like Huck Finn, literal or symbolic orphans — these "Kids" are one and all a terribly violent bunch. America's romance with such brutal heroes as Billy the Kid would seem to indicate that we both desire this deadly innocence and recognize its dangers.

To see the pattern of this American myth in John Wayne, one need only examine a handful of the actor's great Westerns. "Stagecoach" (1939), the story of the Ringo Kid's quest for vengeance against the killer of his father and brother, is a brilliant early example. Set in Monument Valley — one of the unmistakable settings for "Indian Country" in Westerns — the film shows in its opening title sequence a sharply silhouetted cavalry patrol followed a moment later by the ghostly shadows of Apaches. As the opening shot fades, the shadows of the Indians become weirdly transparent and finally dissipate entirely into the rocky backdrop. Director John Ford's subtle message is that this is the cusp of a historical moment called the frontier. The fading silhouettes of the Indians signify the final disappearance of the Vanishing American, still a lingering threat and impediment to inevitable civilization—a threat articulated by a one-word telegram received in the opening scene: "Geronimo."

Civilization itself is represented in "Stagecoach" by, among other elements, both the proper wife who has come to rugged Arizona to join her husband and the corrupt banker who mouths such platitudes as "America for Americans" and "What's good for the banks is good for the country." This civilization is inexorable; the time of wild Apaches and rugged individualists like Ringo is ending. In the second scene of the film, we see a citizens' committee ejecting undesirable elements, a drunken doctor and a prostitute, from their raw Arizona town. Unacceptable to the hypocritical social conscience of the town, both characters will turn out to have sound hearts, and one, the prostitute Dallas, will be given the chance to reclaim her innocence and start anew with John Wayne, the Ringo Kid.

Ringo has escaped from prison to pursue his murderous quest, but he is quickly arrested by a sympathetic sheriff. However, as the quintessential American hero, Ringo cannot be contained by mundane law. A radical innocent, even projecting a nonsexual aura in his courtship of the demure ex-prostitute, Dallas, Ringo is freed by the sheriff to execute his personal justice by shooting his family's killers. Like the American hero he is, Ringo is godlike in his freedom and willingness to deal out justice. That his quest ends in "Lordsburg" underscores this aspect of his character. In the end, Ringo is set free by the sheriff to begin a new life with Dallas on Ringo's ranch somewhere "across the border." The couple depart from Lordsburg with the rehabilitated doctor's benediction: "Well, they're saved from the blessings of civilization." The American hero is always saved from civilization, always moving across the border, always lighting out for the Territory ahead of the rest. Like the Ringo Kid, such a hero takes on qualities of the vanishing American—the romantic but doomed Indian—whose time is over. The message is that the Territory must inevitably give way before necessary civilization, and the uncivilized (non-European) values of Kid and Indian can exist only beyond the border of the imagination, not in the real world. It is doubly ironic, however, that the isolated "Kid" is associated with the Indian, for in traditional Native American cultures elders rather than youths are revered, and the individual is of far less significance than family, clan, and community.

In "Stagecoach," John Wayne was a young man playing a young man's role. He embodied the possibility of starting over, of sloughing off the corrupt past (for Ringo, prison) and reclaiming innocence. The process of reclamation is intensely violent. The ambiguity that might logically spring from this paradox is not apparent in the character of Ringo, however. He begins the film as an innocent and seems unchanged in the end. In that early film, the Apaches are for the most part an off-stage menace, symbolizing the undercurrent of violence always threatening to rise up and overwhelm the uncivil West. When for an instant the camera focuses on Geronimo (actor Chief White Horse), on a bluff looking down at the moving stagecoach, the face reflects an introspective dignity and strength. From an Indian perspective, it is a face that inspires respect and confidence; from a white perspective, it inspires fear.

In "The Cowboys" (1972), John Wayne is no longer young. Deeply scarred for life, Wayne's character of Will Anderson seems at first glance to refute the crucial aspect of the American myth that insists upon a Fountain of Youth, an eternal belief in new beginnings and endless possibility. That there can be no new beginning, no regeneration for Will is suggested in his two long-dead sons, whose graves he visits. "They went bad on me," Will says, adding, "Or I went bad on them." It is the future, the quintessence of the American Dream, that seems to have "gone bad" on Will Anderson. At sixty years of age, he must now get a herd of 1,500 cattle to market 400 miles away simply to ensure that his wife will be provided for after he is dead. The American Dream has given way to social security.

When he discovers that every adult male in his area has run off in search of El Dorado, the dream of easy gold, Will is forced to hire a gaggle of boys to move the herd. The boys, only one of whom is over fifteen years old, represent extreme innocence. Not one of them has even seen a black man before, and they are quick to declare that the black man, Nightlinger, is "the same as us, except for that color," a similarity Nightlinger angrily rejects, pointing out that he is a man and they are boys. The boys are Will's chance to live beyond himself, symbolically to start anew. As Nightlinger, the trail-drive's suggestively named black cook, says to Will, "You got another chance." When Will replies, "They're not mine," Nightlinger adds, "They could be."

In the end, the boys are indeed Will's. After he is shot in a very brutal scene, Will gasps to Nightlinger, "Summer's over," a nice allusion to the coming fall—a time of harvest, of death—and the inevitable fall from innocence awaiting the boys. However, Will's last words are addressed to the boys: "Every man wants his children to be better'n he was. You are." Clearly, they are symbolically children of this iconic American hero, and in being so they allow Will to defy death, to live on.

The boys prove themselves his heirs by coming of age as they kill Will's murderers, who are led by the purely evil Asa Watts (brilliantly played by Bruce Dern), and by reclaiming the stolen cattle herd. In a highly symbolic gesture, the boys begin to kill the villains one by one. As each bad guy dies, one of the boys puts on the bad guy's clothing and temporarily assumes the villain's place with the herd. The message is clear: The boys are becoming like the American hero, Will Anderson—and like the earlier Ringo

Kid—by going outside the law and executing their own justice. In so doing, however, as the appropriated clothing suggests, they also partake of the evil of those they kill. If they become like Will, they also become like their evil adversaries. Killing as initiation rite is further underscored in the film's climactic scene as the camera closes in on each of the boys in succession killing one of the rustlers. In the lethal children, the film underscores the nature of the Western hero. He is a *cowboy*, a *kid* like all his namesakes in Western lore. The Western hero is not supposed to grow up, just as the West and America itself are not supposed to grow old. When that happens it seems, as Will says, that something has gone bad.

Near the end of "The Cowboys," Nightlinger and the boys search for Will's grave to place a marker there. But the grave has been erased by rain—suggestive of regeneration and new beginning—and the stone must be left randomly on the wide prairie. Thus Will has simply become a part of all America, nourishing the common soil. Nightlinger's eulogy underscores the point: "This may seem like a lonesome place to leave him. But he's not alone. Because many of his kind rest here with him. The prairie was like a mother to Mr. Anderson." Will Anderson, the cowboy hero, was born of America. Symbolically, he is also the father of us all.

Native Americans were from the beginning the fly in the New World ointment for invading Europeans. How could the true American hero, the new-made man, maintain his giant stride across the continent when he kept running into communities of people who had already inhabited that so-called New World sometimes for tens of thousands of years? For Native American Indians, the New World was a very old world. Furthermore, to the Indian the very idea of the American hero was absurd. While the hero must operate alone, ahead of the rest, for the Indian the community was essential to both physical and psychological survival. To be isolated, like all those wandering cowboy heroes, was to have no identity and to perish. To be alone, outside the tribe, was not to be heroic but to have been, in Indian terms, "thrown away." Finally, how could the American hero maintain the aura of innocence necessary in this new Eden when he had to drive the Indians from their ancestral homes and murder countless thousands in the process? It was an ugly, unconscionable business troubling even to an American society bent on cultural and physical genocide for Indians.

In the movies of John Wayne—the actor who not only endorsed the witch-hunts of McCarthyism but also in a *Playboy* magazine interview justified the extermination of Indians—America found the answer to such an uncomfortable dilemma. The answer, of course, is to assume that the Native American is on the verge of extinction, the uncomfortable business of genocide practically over and forgotten. The ugly facts of extermination become merely an unfortunate part of the past that, in the American tradition, can be forgotten as once again we reinvent ourselves as a kinder, gentler nation. As an added benefit, on the brink of extinction the Indian is seen as no longer either a real threat to the European invader or significant enough to stake a convincing claim to the continent.

Once it is assumed that the Indian neither threatens white civilization nor possesses a meaningful claim to property, America is finally able to look at the Indian sympathetically. The Indian then becomes a historical artifact of distinct value. The role of the white man is now to learn as much as possible from the Indian—that is, to become as much as possible *like* the Indian without *being* the Indian—before the race of Native Americans disappears with the setting sun. It is at that stage of cowboys-and-Indians history that John Wayne enters the picture. At that moment in history when full appropriation of everything Indian, including not only land but every cultural vestige that may be of value to the white world, seems justifiably inevitable, the Indian can finally be pitied, protected, and emulated safely.

In the '90s, Kevin Costner's "Dances with Wolves" illustrated this convergence very clearly, as Costner's protagonist goes into Indian country, desperate to see the frontier "before it's gone," strips himself bare, and appropriates all that he can of the Indian. Finally, as the U.S. Cavalry is about to corner and slaughter the remaining Sioux, Dunbar returns to the white world bearing the recovered white female. The Indian, Costner's audience understands by the end of "Dances with Wolves," is a doomed artifact, and the audience is invited to shed a crocodile tear for the lost people and lost time. However, that which is valuable and retrievable in Sioux culture has been absorbed and thus salvaged by Costner's character to make the white world a better place; even the symbolic threat of miscegenation has been removed as the protagonist returns bearing the recovered white woman.

Among contemporary films, "Dances with Wolves" illustrates this pattern of thought most clearly, but it is a pattern obvious in the films of John Marion Morrison Wayne. A crucial difference between Costner's character of Dunbar in "Dances with Wolves" and the John Wayne hero, however, is that at the end of his film Dunbar returns to civilization. It is evident that he has never really deserted that other world. For the Wayne hero, on the other hand, there can be no place outside of "Indian country" — even when Indian country is devoid of Indians. The Wayne hero, too, is an artifact. It was this discovery that provided the greatest roles for an aging John Wayne, in such films as "True Grit" (1969) and "The Shootist " (1976).

As Rooster Cogburn in "True Grit," Wayne is a man out of time and place, beyond civilized law, dealing out violent justice according to his own values. To find room where his kind of hero can operate, Rooster must leave civilization and go into "Indian Territory" where, as Mark

Twain suggested, the "sound heart" can overrule the "deformed conscience." In the civilized world, Rooster complains about "pettifogging lawyers" and serves a "writ" on a rat by shooting the animal. In essence, John Wayne is playing the same role he played in "Stagecoach" almost half a century earlier. He is still charmingly innocent, offering not the faintest hint of sexual threat to the attractive young woman, Mattie Ross, whom he takes into the Territory. Mattie, who dresses in asexual clothing and constantly challenges the men in masculine terms, is called "Baby Sister" by Rooster. It is clear that it is not the hero but his environment that has changed. The marked difference between the two versions of the hero in "Stagecoach" and "True Grit" arises out of John Wayne's comically self-conscious parody in the role of Rooster. Civilization has engulfed him and age has shockingly tracked him down, and Wayne camps his way through the role, a charming (though still lethal) drunk.

Like the archetypal hero he is, Rooster has no family, living his liminal existence with an old Chinese man, whom he introduces as his father, and a cat he calls his nephew. Rooster's encounter with a mixed-blood Indian policeman in the Territory is marked by mutual respect and familiarity — they seem to recognize that as marginal figures they are much alike. In the film's final scene, Mattie Ross, whom he has aided in avenging her father's murder, tells him, "You're getting too old and too fat to be jumping over fences," and our last view is of Rooster defying time by jumping his horse over a distant fence. Just like the Ringo Kid, he's heading across a border into a place where he can live beyond civilization. Where he's really headed, however, is suggested in Mattie's invitation to him to be buried in her family's plot. Only beyond this world, which he must traverse alone, can the American hero find a family.

"The Shootist" (1976) was John Wayne's last film. In it he plays John Bernard Books, a legendary gunman dying of cancer. A reprise of his life's role, the film pays tribute to John Wayne the actor, giving him the opportunity to close out his career with the enormous, tragic dignity befitting the great American hero that he was. After a ritualistic cleansing, Books goes forth to die by violence on his birthday in a manner he himself has determined. That his name is Books tells us volumes about the John Wayne hero: As his name announces, he is a product of our collective self-imagining, an animated text that tells the story of America. Most incredible in all of this is that Marion Morrison did, in fact, give himself over to the European-American imagination to be reshaped, reborn into a fictive hero with his off-screen self shaped entirely by the camera's view. In the end, Marion Morrison was John Wayne, through and through—a most strange kind of self-sacrifice.

BARAZANI

YESHAYAHU KOREN

Yeshayahu Koren was born in 1940 in Kfar Saba, Israel. He studied philosophy and Hebrew literature at the Hebrew University in Jerusalem.

Mr. Koren is the author of the books (in Hebrew) *Letter in the Sands* and *Midday Funeral*. The following selection is from the book *Doves Don't Fly at Night*, a collection of short stories published by Hakibbutz Hameuchad/Siman Kriah, Tel Aviv.

Mr. Koren lives in Jerusalem.

It was our third posting to Lebanon, and I wanted to go to the collection point with Barazani. I arrived at his metalwork shop and pushed open the door. A cloud of dust assaulted my nose. A sharp rustling cut the air: The notice hanging on the door had torn. The shop was quiet, but muffled voices came from the far end of the room.

I sat on an overturned crate and waited. I didn't like going into the storeroom on my own. Barazani had only taken me there once. A variety of coins were arranged on the shelves of an old glass-fronted cupboard: from the Bar-Kochba period, from some town in Germany or Italy where they had once used Jewish money, from Persia, Iraq, from the British Mandate, and coins dating from the first years of statehood.

Next to me stood a low table. Beneath a cracked sheet of glass were notes, newspaper clippings, and faded pictures of soccer players. Scattered on top were old and new soccer pool forms, some with calculations scribbled in pencil. A few old records lay on one corner, a half cup of cold coffee on top. Yonah Barazani, as usual, had forgotten to finish it. Oily rags and dirty, sweat-soaked clothes were strewn on the floor. I was thirsty. Barazani emerged from the storeroom and said: "Let's go. The car's outside."

"Why do we need the car?" I asked. "Everyone's gathering at the city park; it's less than five minutes' walk."

"I've decided to take the Volvo," said Barazani. "Like the good old days."

"You're crazy." I set my suitcase down. "Lebanon's not like the good old days when you could drive to maneuvers, or even to the front. No one'll let you through."

"Last time I found a way."

"Look here, Barazani," I said quietly, "I'm telling you you can't do it, and don't forget I'm your platoon sergeant."

"Don't give me that crap. If we only did what we were told, where would we be today?"

"I'm not joking. We've got enough problems as it is."

"Everything's ready. I went shopping yesterday. Our stuff's already in the boot. Come on, gimme your case and stop acting like a child."

Barazani was the oldest soldier in the company, about forty-nine. A pepper-and-salt mustache. Brown face, strong and lined. He picked up my suitcase and turned to the door. "Now who the hell's gone and torn my notice?"

It was a schedule of the Betar Jerusalem soccer team's games for the next few weeks. Trying to mend the tear, he said: "I can pass up the game week after next; it's a weak team and there won't be any problems, even if it is an away game. But this coming Saturday—make a note! I'm getting leave. We're playing Hapoel Kfar-Saba, and we've got to get back the points we lost in the last round."

I knew he was actually demanding that I give him leave. Barazani was a fanatical Betar fan. He contributed money to the club, took noisemakers to the games, and came home hoarse after every match. The only thing he didn't believe in, he told me once, was "that business of releasing doves. Doves don't mix with soccer."

"Why not?" I asked. There was a heap of old programs and photocopies, rusty screws, and lengths of pipe next to the door.

"Because they don't. I have arguments about it in the club too." He pushed the pile of rubbish aside with his foot, and an open magazine fell against my suitcase.

"You'll get your leave," I said. "But now let's go get on the bus like normal human beings."

He locked the door, descended the stone steps to the sidewalk, and shoved my case into the trunk of the car. Our weapons, which were lying there, he transferred to the back seat. A police siren wailed in the main street. From the falafel stand floated an aroma of oil mixed with onions, garlic, and spices. Yonah paused for a moment and said: "Let's flip a coin. If you win—we won't take the car. We'll go by bus."

I knew him and his coins. He was an expert at flipping two-mille coins from the Mandate period. He knew exactly how to swoop his hand, catch the coin, and win. I lit a cigarette and said: "What do you say?"

He rummaged in his pocket and asked: "Tree or Palestine?"*

"Pali," I said.

He went on rummaging, and finally produced a greenish copper coin. Spinning it in front of my eyes, he snapped his thumb and flipped the coin into the air. The coin flew up, turned over, almost hit a branch of the tree in whose shade we were standing, and began spinning down. I saw his lips tighten. His gleaming blue eyes followed its progress. His shoulders were hunched, his hand outstretched, tensed. Two feet before it reached him, Barazani swept his arm in an arc like a reaper, waited, and seized the coin. There was silence. His face was guarded. Straightening up, he opened his fist. Seven leaves peeped through the greenish patina of the coin.

"Okay," said Barazani, "We're taking the car." It was tree.

A cold wind blew down the alley. We climbed into the Volvo. He turned on the heater as the car turned onto the main street and approached the collection point. "What are you doing?" I asked.

"Go and see if they've all shown up." The way he always tried to run my life was annoying, but I couldn't be angry with him.

Two of the buses had already left. The last one was still waiting for late-comers.

---

*The British Mandate equivalent of heads or tails.

"Actually, everyone's here," said the CSM, the company sergeant major. "We'll pick up a few men on the way and in Nakura. What about you guys?"

"We'll get there in the Volvo," said Barazani.

"You'll have to leave it in Rosh Hanikra."

Barazani said nothing.

The CSM mounted the steps of the bus, did a head count, and said: "Apart from Shlomi, everyone's here."

"Shlomi'll be late," I said.

"How d'you know?"

"As usual. Problems with his girlfriend." But even as I spoke, I saw Shlomi running down the street, his pack bouncing on his back. A brown boot dangled by one lace from the pack.

In the corner of the windshield, over the dashboard, was an old family snapshot. Barazani with fewer lines on his face, black hair. His wife, plump, long frizzy hair, lips thick and dark with lipstick, face smooth and fair. Three children. The oldest, a boy of thirteen, straight blond hair falling over blue eyes. The daughter, in a red plaid dress, hugging her little brother, who was plump with a round face and curly brown hair.

Barazani looked at the picture, and the car skidded to the side of the road. The wheels bounced on gravel; when they steadied on the road again, Barazani put a cassette in the tape player—dance music from an army program. He looked at the picture again. The windshield misted over, and I turned on the wipers for a moment. Barazani turned them off and pointed to his older son in the picture. "Seventeen and a half already," he said. "In six months he'll be going to the army, dammit. It's him who tapes these cassettes for me. And look at Shlomi. Out of the army for a year already. Don't he look like a kid still, with that hair in his eyes, always turning up in the same old pair of pants?"

"Come off it," I said. "Shlomi's been on civvie street a year already and he hasn't even found a job yet. Trouble with his girlfriend all the time."

"And we haven't got trouble? That's exactly why I like him." Barazani laughed loudly. "Never mind if he does support Hapoel Kfar-Saba, who took the cup away from us in '75. I'll still get him for that." He took a cigarette out of the pack in his khaki shirt pocket .

"He doesn't remember anything about it. He was still a kid then."

"That's just why he remembers. No kid would ever forget a game like that."

I pressed the cigarette lighter on the dashboard, and when the coils turned red I lit his cigarette. Barazani inhaled deeply and coughed, and I put the lighter back in place. "Pick up your foot," he suddenly yelled. Ash fell from the cigarette onto his trousers. Smoke blurred his face and stung my eyes. "Can't you see you're stepping on my program?" I picked up the purple photocopy and threw it onto the back seat. It fell onto weeklies, old sports magazines, an empty plastic bag from a department store, and an open wooden box. In the box, among screws, pliers, screwdrivers, were a few beer cans, some empty, some full. Barazani leaned back to pick up one of them and offered it to me. "Have a beer," he said.

We arrived at the Rosh Hanikra border post and stopped to get something hot to drink at one of the stands. Trucks and command cars, tanks and M-113s were crowded into the parking lot on the cliff overlooking the sea. Soldiers milled around and disappeared into the narrow lanes between the vehicles: private cars, Jeeps, officers' Landrovers, and big Mercedeses with green Lebanese license plates. An MP was moving down the lanes checking entry permits. We came back from the kiosk. The MP stopped Barazani and said: "Where's your permit?"

"Hang on a minute," said Barazani. He opened the car

door and rummaged around in the glove compartment. Then, making sure that the MP wasn't looking, he pulled his call-up papers out of his shirt pocket and held them out.

"That's your call-up papers. Where's your permit?" The MP leaned against the car. His eyes were dim with sleep.

"What? That's not it? Our company commander told us to meet them on the Kasmiyyeh Bridge. I gotta get moving. This is the tenth time I've gone through here."

"But that's not a permit. Anyway, you know private cars aren't allowed in." The MP scratched the ginger beard fringing his face. His uniform blouse was old, and there was a pale patch on the sleeve.

"Every day you change the damn rules," said Barazani. Cars were honking behind us. "This ain't the first time I've gone through here."

"Move aside," said the MP.

"How the hell am I supposed to move?" said Barazani. Cars and buses full of soldiers blocked our way in all directions.

"Move aside," said the MP again. He signaled to the driver of the Jeep behind us.

"I want to talk to the checkpoint commander," said Barazani.

His cigarette was getting shorter, the ash longer, almost touching his lips. Barazani took another drag. The ash reddened and fell onto his old shoes.

"That won't help you," said the MP. "At the checkpoint they check again, and they won't let you through."

"Let me try," said Barazani.

"So they can say you made a fool of me?" said the MP.

In spite of the cold wind, I thought I saw beads of sweat glittering between the lines on Barazani's forehead. He took the cigarette pack out of his pocket, but it was empty. Tossing it away, he suddenly smiled and said: "Okay. You have to do your job. So clear the way for me at least, so's I can get out of here." He came up to me and said softly: "It won't work. We'll have to go back."

"Let's wait for our buses," I said.

"By the time those buses get here, we'll go crazy. If they want us to screw them, it's their own lookout."

He went back to the kiosk to buy cigarettes, and I rummaged idly in the glove compartment. A bit of a newspaper clipping was stuck on the inside of the compartment door: "A few days after the war, among the crowds of Israelis flooding Hebron was a well-known Jerusalem antique dealer. Next to the Tomb of the Patriarchs he got into a cab and asked the driver to take him to an antique shop. The cab drove through the alleys, and after a while it seemed to the Jerusalem dealer that they had left Hebron behind them and were already in the heart of the Judean desert. He panicked and asked the cab driver: Where are we going? The Hebronite looked at the elegant Jerusalem antique dealer and said: I didn't think an ordinary antique shop would interest you. I wanted to take you to the place where they make them."

Clouds accompanied the waves advancing in the sea, opposite the cliffs of Rosh Hanikra. But what with the heater and my parka and the smell of smoke filling the car, I was hot. I was sweating. There was no point getting out and waiting for the buses. They always drove slowly and stopped at kiosks at all the junctions. There were few alternatives. Barazani had won after all.

He got into the car, lit another cigarette, and switched on the tape again. Lonely, late-night tunes filled the car. We returned to the northern road intersection. And even before we passed them I felt homesick for the green fields, for the straight avenues of trees in the orchards, for the round, concrete reservoir on top of the hill. Near Hanita we turned off toward the border. The fence was completely broken down. An occasional car passed us with a train of dust accompanying it and then dying down and filling the low bushes. I looked at the photograph of Barazani's family again, and it too seemed to be covered with dust. In the distance, on the crest of a hill, was an Arab village whose name I didn't know. At an abandoned school beside the road children were driving an old car. They zigzagged jerkily between the trees and a broken basket-ball hoop. The songs were slow. Barazani hummed something. The jolting motion put me to sleep. I dozed off.

"La Comparsita!" I woke to a yell that filled the car. My feet were sweating. I stretched, yawned, and looked at Barazani. He turned toward me, and laughed. His cheek-bones stuck out, his lips were clamped shut. Again he looked at the picture on the windshield and wiped the dust off with a finger. The tape stopped. The windows were closed, and the heater gave off an exhausting heat. I too lit a cigarette.

"I like old tunes," said Barazani.

"And I don't even know them," I said. I didn't yet know that "La Comparsita" was an old tango, dating to the for-ties or earlier.

A reconnaissance Jeep came flying toward us. In the wake of the column of dust it raised came an old military ambulance. A safari command car, with helmeted soldiers sitting back to back, drove behind the ambulance. In the sky were black and gray clouds, and a north wind beat against the windshield in dry waves.

"An ambulance means there's still hope," said Barazani.

"Where do you get that from?"

"They took Yoel away by helicopter."

"Yes," I said, "and it was too late. But there isn't always a helicopter available."

A few drops of rain fell. Heavy drops. They fell on the dust that covered the hood. Barazani mumbled something, his eyes fixed on the road; it sounded to me like "La Comparsita" again.

We crossed a low bridge. Barren cherry trees grew thick on either side. Barazani bent down and pulled an M-16 from under the seat. The car swerved off the road, and he stopped for a minute. A bird crashed into the front of the hood and went on flying. Barazani put the M-16 down next to him and opened the window. The bird flew over our heads and he said: "Put your Uzi on your knees."

I didn't answer, and he said: "It's no joke. Put it on your knees."

In the distance, I saw the green domes of the mosques of Nabatiyeh. The Uzi was lying on the back seat, among the clutter. I turned round and pulled it toward me. When I turned back, the picture of Barazani's family loomed in front of me again, with the straight blond hair of the oldest son.

"He really does look like Shlomi," I said suddenly. A dark oil stain spread over my lap from the Uzi. Barazani too looked at the picture and grinned.

A terrible stink assailed us. We were in Ansar. Passing the checkpoint on the outskirts of the village, we drove round the prison camp. The wind kept blowing into our faces the smell of the sewage that ran through the camp.

A half-track drove past. We shut the windows and Barazani said: "Maybe we can stop in Nabatiyeh and do a bit of shopping."

"We should stay put and start getting organized," I said.

"You've got time till they arrive. Just getting out of the bottleneck in Nakura takes hours. Look at my shoes. I have to pick up a couple of pairs here."

The camp commandant, a gray-haired guy with a thin, gray mustache, was walking round between the huts. When he saw us, he said: "Hello, Barazani. I see you brought the Volvo again. One day you'll get it in the neck. Hide it in the back, behind the detention tent."

"Where's our billets?" asked Barazani.

"Over there, at the end of the camp. In the precast blocks."

"Blocks, shmocks. Is there anything hot to drink?" said Barazani. We drove there. Barazani walked around the precast huts and stopped at the next to last. "We'll take this one. It's at the end and not at the end. And we can park the car between these two shmocks." He got back in the car, parked it, and opened the trunk.

The buses arrived.

Shlomi got out first and ran toward us. "I have to get leave on Saturday." He was panting. His eyes were red. His hair was wild and covered with a thin veil of dust. The M-16 was hung carelessly from his shoulder, and he held a newspaper in his hand.

"Hold your horses," I said. "We're not organized yet, and you're already talking about leave."

"I'll do whatever you say. But I've got to get leave on Saturday," said Shlomi. His face was taut and his hair ravaged by the wind.

"What's wrong?" I asked. But he was silent. When we were in Lebanon the first time, too, he had asked for leave. Then he had a story about problems with his girlfriend, and it was true. She was in France at the time, and it really was a problem.

"Is she back?"

"Long ago. And I have to get leave. Believe me."

"I heard you," I said. "But you're not the only one. We'll take you into account."

He wanted to get his pack from the bus, but everyone got off at once, pushing and shoving, and he stood to one side, next to the pile of gear being unloaded from the top of the bus. The wind ruffled his newspaper. He tried to fold the pages, but one of them tore. Packs were thrown roughly on the ground. Someone asked, shouting, if they couldn't put them down properly so they wouldn't get muddy, but no one paid any attention. Only Shlomi went over and took a cigarette from him. Succeeding in lighting it with the third match, he held the cigarette with two fingers as if it were the first he had ever smoked.

Barazani got the hut organized. He found an old ammunition box and stood it next to the bed. Then he took out a tattered notebook and began making calculations on the coming Saturday's soccer games.

"Filling in the soccer pools?" I asked.

"It's got nothing to do with the pools," he said. "The pools is a different system altogether."

Afterward we cleaned our weapons, and in the evening we went on our first patrol. Driving through Nabatiyeh, Barazani said again that he wanted to buy shoes.

"You're out of line," I said.

"What's wrong?"

"How can you go out on patrol in civilian shoes? You should have worn boots."

"Boots don't fit my feet," he said. His shoes were scuffed and shabby, the uppers coming apart from the soles. Tiny thorns clung to his socks and the hems of his trousers.

The next morning we sent details to man the checkpoints, and the rest of the men were allowed to sleep till noon. Barazani woke early and drove to Nabatiyeh to buy shoes for the children and himself and slippers for his wife. From the distance, on the roofs of the houses, I saw black flags and big pictures of some imam of theirs who had disappeared in Libya, and I remembered the way they had whipped themselves in the streets the year before.

"It's some holy day of theirs," I said to Barazani. "You shouldn't have gone there."

"Look," he said, "as long as they're selling, I'm buying. The shoes are comfortable, and they're cheap too." Shlomi also got out of the Volvo. He was carrying a blouse embroidered in red, green, and white.

"He needs leave on Saturday too," said Barazani.

"He told me. But there's no end to it. Anyway, this time I think they're going to do it by company. Is something wrong?"

"You mean you don't know?" said Barazani. Shlomi went into the hut, and Barazani and I stood next to the Volvo.

"What can be wrong with her?"

"Let's not talk about it."

A command car carrying prisoners with wispy beards drove past on the muddy, red dirt road. Planes flew overhead. A little rain fell, but the wind kept blowing, and the stink from the sewage canal of the prison camp reached us in waves.

In the evening the CSM came and asked us to evacuate the hut. They wanted to set up the CC's office in it. Barazani refused, but suddenly he laughed and said: "Tree or Palestine?" "Pali," said the CSM and sat on the ammunition box beside Barazani's bed. Barazani took out a coin, flipped it high in the air, crouched down, and readied his hand. When the coin approached his chest, I saw his tense face and I knew that the CSM had lost. Barazani caught the coin, opened his fist, and said: "Tree! You've had it!"

The CSM stood up and leaned against the door frame, his lips twisted. Barazani said: "Never mind. You lost, but we'll do you a favor and get out anyway. The CC's the CC, any way you look at it." The CSM was silent, and a soldier arrived at a run and said: "The deputy CC said it's okay. They've found a better place."

In the evening Shlomi went to the phone, and his unintelligible shouts reached the big Indian-pattern tent that served as mess hall and bordered the operations tent. I was playing cards. Barazani was drinking coffee and working out his calculations on the Saturday soccer matches. He made notes on the margins of a newspaper and glanced occasionally at his tattered notebook. Standing up, he walked around with the coffee cup in his hand. Then he returned to the table and said: "There's nothing for it; they need my voice there on Saturday. I have to get leave."

A command car drove past. There was the sound of an explosion in the distance. Nobody moved. Only the soldier on guard at the entrance to the camp lowered his gun from his shoulder. The big oil stain on my trousers was caked with dust.

On Thursday, the patrol force set out, and two checkpoint details relieved the previous shifts at the camp intersection and the exit from Nabatiyeh. It was already ten p.m. The generator hummed. No one had gone to sleep yet.

We sat in the Indian-pattern tent. The CSM, the cook, and the CO's driver were playing cards, and the CSM asked me if I wanted to take a hand. "In a minute," I said. Two young soldiers were sitting next to a dangling naked bulb, drinking beer, reading yesterday's newspaper, and arguing. "The place for history lessons is the university, not here," a tall soldier said to them. His hands in the pockets of an oil-stained parka, he stood at the entrance looking at the black orange grove covering the opposite hill. Then he turned, took out a letter, and gave it to Barazani.

Barazani was sitting on a long wooden bench. He already was holding a bunch of letters and soccer pool forms he had been asked to deliver in Israel. Only three people had been given leave, and Barazani had been granted a special pass in view of his veteran status in the unit. He had promised to bring back from his shop special stands for the machine guns at the checkpoints, so that they would be off the ground and ready for firing. The old-timers remembered that in the Six-Day War, during the alert before the fighting broke out, Barazani had provided similar stands for the machine guns on the command cars. "Convenient for sitting, observing, and reacting efficiently," said the CC, justifying the pass to himself. "All for some lousy soccer game," I said to myself, and saw the tattered notebook sticking out of Barazani's pocket.

Shlomi sat down opposite me. He didn't touch the coffee in front of him, and he tried to persuade me that he had to go on leave. I said that I had nothing against his going, but it had already been decided. "Think about the men who've got families," I said.

"They've got families," he said. "Right."

I didn't know what more to say to him. "Speak to Barazani," I said.

"Barazani's not part of the quota," called the CSM, raising his cards to his eyes, "he's an exception."

"So what?" I said. "You can substitute one exception for another."

"Impossible. That would mean that four men went on leave."

"Barazani's not a human being as far as you're concerned?"

The company clerk arrived and said to the CSM, "The CC wants you."

"What's up?"

"We have to bring the inventory up to date."

"So bring it up to date, dammit. Can't you do anything without me?" But he shuffled his cards together, slammed them down on the table, and left the tent.

Barazani shoved the letters and soccer forms into the pocket of his parka and went over to Shlomi. "You want to go instead of me?"

"No," said Shlomi. "I don't want anyone to give up his leave for me."

"It was decided that only three men are going," I said. "You can go next week." Then I added, "So call her and get it over."

"I call her all the time," said Shlomi. "But I can't talk to her on the phone."

"'It was decided that only three men are going,'" the tall soldier repeated, "and that's why only four are going."

"You'll go next week." I repeated to Shlomi.

He was quiet and then blurted: "Next week's too late."

"Dammit," I said, "You've only just been demobbed. Have you already forgotten what being in the army means?"

"I haven't forgotten. In the army I'd have gone AWOL. Here with all those old men I wouldn't feel right."

"I'll talk to the CSM again," I said.

I went over to the operations tent. The CSM was busy fixing the inventory. I could never understand what was so difficult about adding up the number of soldiers in the unit and getting one clear result. The clerk copied the lists; the CSM corrected them, erased, added on, and changed the order; then the clerk copied them out again. By platoons, by squads, by the alphabet, by rank. And whenever he was asked how many men were in the company, the CSM would reply, "About 79; I still have to check."

"Get off my back," he said, when I mentioned Shlomi. "He's a child."

"So let him have his candy first," I said, "and then he can wait until his turn comes round again."

"From your platoon, Barazani's going. It's your headache. I don't give a damn who goes. Just let me know so's I can bring the inventory up to date."

I went back to the mess tent. Barazani was roaming round among the tables. The wind blew through the tent flaps and covered his suitcase with pale dust. Shlomi stood next to the the corner tent pole and his head brushed the canvas. The two soldiers who were reading the newspaper were still arguing: "We should never have come in here in the first place."

"What difference does it make? Now we're in up to our necks. Even if we get out."

"What's that supposed to mean?"

"It's not supposed to mean anything. But that's the way it is."

I didn't want to talk to Barazani, but when I sat down he

came up to me.

"What're we going to do about Shlomi?" I said.

"Let him go. What difference does it make? Who cares?"

"I can't. It's not just ongoing operations. There's an alert on too. They say we're gonna stick it to them good and proper tomorrow night."

"As long as we don't stick it in too far. Afterward we'll have a hard time getting it out again."

"They say it'll be the last push."

"Every day they say something different."

"I dunno, but it looks like they need everyone. To stop up all the gaps."

Barazani said nothing. He tore a little strip of paper from the folded, creased sports magazine in his hand. "Nothing'll come of it," he said. "Don't you know them by now? They've always got some reason." He bent over his suitcase and tucked the magazine under the handle.

A cloud of dust rose from the corner of the tent. Shlomi approached and said in an undertone: "Did he say anything to you?"

"Enough!" I yelled. "You can't go. Only if somebody else lets you go instead of him. Forget it."

There was a noise of M-113 engines outside. The patrol was back. "The checkpoints'll have to be relieved soon," I thought. A strong wind beat at the tent flaps. It was cold and dry. The CSM returned and resumed his place at the card table. The tall soldier yelled into the telephone. Shlomi stood at the entrance, huddled in his parka.

"To hell with it," said Barazani suddenly. "It's him or me, right?"

"It doesn't have to be," I said.

"So let's flip a coin." He stood up, suddenly laughed, and said: "Let them manage without me." Then he turned to Shlomi. "Keep smiling, Shlomi," he said in English, "and don't take everything to heart. So what do you want: tree or Palestine?"

126

"Pali."

"Damn," said Barazani. He rummaged in his trouser pockets and in the end came up with his old coin: a two-mille coin from the British Mandate.

Gradually everyone got up and drew closer. Even the card players laid their cards face down on the table and joined the circle. I knew what the outcome would be, but I kept quiet. The CSM touched Shlomi's shoulder and said: "Why should he flip the coin? You do it." But Shlomi pushed his hands into his parka pockets and didn't say a word.

Barazani's eyes darted round anxiously. He looked from side to side, wiped the corner of his mouth, and moved the coin around inside his fist.

"He's cheating," called someone. But Barazani had already flipped the coin high into the air with his thumb. I knew what was going to happen, and probably the old-timers who knew Barazani did too. I saw his tense face when he crouched, his hand on a split-second alert next to his knees.

Shlomi stood outside the circle. The coin fell and came parallel with Barazani's chest, but before it could touch him he reached out and snatched it. His head was thrust forward, his eyes darted round his audience. He turned around, and when he saw Shlomi he opened his fist in a flash, and said: "Pali, dammit; you've got leave."

There was a noise in the tent. In the distance a few bursts of fire were heard. Flames spread over one of the hills. Shlomi laughed, grinned, and ran to the phone. "Hello, hello," he yelled, and I heard him say, or maybe sing: "I just called to say I love you. I just called to say how much I care." But when he put the receiver down he went back to the tent pole and fine clouds of dust rose from his footsteps. Barazani went up to him and gave him the bunch of letters and soccer forms from his pocket. Shlomi smoked a cigarette. Somebody else was whistling the tune now.

*   *   *

On Friday, at four a.m., they drove off.

Barazani got onto the half-track setting out on the morning patrol. He was wearing the new shoes he had bought in Nabatiyeh. The other pairs he had left on the shelf in the hut, lined up according to size.

He was standing behind the company machine gun, broad, sturdy, unshaven, his eyes burning in the wind. The old balaclava he dragged with him from reserve duty to reserve duty covered his head and forehead. It was cold, and they were all huddled in the faded parkas that were handed down from intake to intake and were covered with oil stains.

They drove out the gate, and before returning to the hut I went back into the mess tent. My mouth was dry from the wind, and I needed something hot to drink. A jug of tea stood on one of the tables, and I took a few sips. Next to the tent pole I saw Shlomi's pack. A gray sweater was tied to the buckles. Inside the folded sweater was a packet with the letters and soccer forms peeping out of it. I looked around, but the·tent was empty.

I went back to the hut. I couldn't close the shutter. The wind beat against it and the hinges creaked. I lay awake, and at about six a.m. I went outside. A soldier came running out of the operations tent. I went inside and heard over the radio that a grenade had been thrown at a half-truck; shots were fired, and there were casualties.

The CSM called the doctor. The ops officer ordered a helicopter to evacuate the wounded. We drove to the scene. Barazani lay on the hood of the half-track, unmoving. The doctor said there was no pulse and that he had been killed on the spot.

The medical orderly straightened his legs and laid his arms along his sides. He opened Barazani's clenched fist. A coin rolled out of it onto the hood and fell on the destroyed ground. I picked up the coin, tossed it from hand to hand. When they let off a smoke grenade to show the helicopter where to land, the smoke spread over us all and rose broad and spiraling into the sky. I blinked my eyes, which were full of tears, and looked at the rusty two-mille coin from the Mandate period, and at the word written on it in English, Hebrew, and Arabic. Both sides of the coin were the same. Palestine.

The helicopter descended noisily. Sand, mud, leaves, scraps of paper, dust, and dirty plastic bags flew into the air. "But there has to be another coin," I shouted at the medical orderly who had emptied the pockets of Barazani's torn and charred uniform. He was standing next to me, looking at the approaching helicopter, his eyes blinking and watering in the wind. "Here," he said in a hoarse voice, and held out the other coin.

It was the other side of the coin. On both sides of the greenish copper was a slender, upright olive branch, with seven leaves spreading from its sides.

Translated from the Hebrew by Dalya Bilu

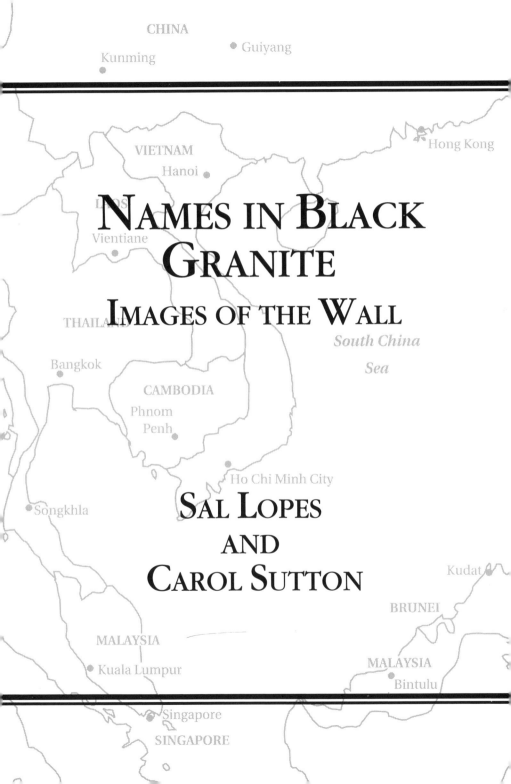

NAMES IN BLACK GRANITE

IMAGES OF THE WALL

SAL LOPES
AND
CAROL SUTTON

Sal Lopes was born in Middletown, Connecticut, and is a professional photographer. He received a Master of Education degree at the University of Hartford.

© 1992 Carol Sutton

Mr. Lopes's photography has appeared in exhibits at the Art Institute of Chicago, the San Francisco Museum of Modern Art, and the International Center of Photography, among others. His images and photographic essays have been published in a number of publications including *Newsweek*, *National Geographic*, and the *New York Times*. Mr. Lopes directed and was the major photographic contributor to the book *The Wall: Images and Offerings from the Vietnam Veterans Memorial*. He was a guest on "Nightline" with Ted Koppel.

Mr. Lopes lives in the Boston area.

Carol Sutton was born in Orlando, Florida. She received a Master of Music degree at the School of Music, Florida State University, and continued her studies in Paris and Boston.

Ms. Sutton is a free-lance writer and editor. She lives in Boston.

© 1993 Sal Lopes

Mr. Lopes and Ms. Sutton are currently working on a forthcoming book, a photojournal of people living with AIDS. The book will be published in spring 1994. A corresponding photographic exhibition will open in early 1994 at the Chrysler Museum in Norfolk, Virginia.

W hen Sal Lopes began photographing the Wall, the word "hero" never entered his mind. What attracted him wasn't the war, which was past, but the present, the aftermath, the living. Many still suffer because of the Vietnam War, and maybe *they* are some of the heroes—those who came home to a country hostile to them because the soldiers who fought were confused with the policy makers who had sent them into combat. Yet they put their lives back together and survived.

In truth, vastly different types of people could be called heroic. Half of being a hero is circumstance. Does the fact that one soldier put his life on the line for another make him more a hero than one who possesses the same degree of bravery but was never in a position to take the same action? Many who opposed the war were heroic as well, their convictions as strong as the convictions of the men and women who made the sacrifice of going to Southeast Asia.

The following images do commemorate the dead. But what captured the photographer's attention most was the living.

You need not have been killed in action to be a casualty of war. The people who visit the memorial illustrate this, from veterans who make regular pilgrimages to the Wall to the woman from the Midwest who went because she heard that the name of someone from her hometown—a boy she never knew—was inscribed there. In between are the mothers and fathers, wives and children, and others with special ties to a name on the Wall.

Nor do you have to have died on foreign soil to be a casualty. Some estimate that as many as 100,000 former soldiers—*twice the number of names etched on the Wall*—have taken their own lives since they came back. It is a staggering statistic.

But Lopes did not visit the Wall to photograph heroes, living or dead. His first trip to the nation's newest and, on the day it was dedicated, most controversial shrine was to pay a debt to four close friends who lost their lives in Vietnam. After that, he returned to the Wall again and again to photograph people connecting to the Wall and to each other through shared grief.

The city of Washington contains a multitude of memorials, yet the Wall is unlike any other. In 1979 a Vietnam veteran named Jan Scruggs recognized that the sacrifice of thousands and thousands of Americans had never been acknowledged and would in all likelihood be forgotten. He decided that a memorial was needed, and he said from the start that four conditions had to be met: (1) The name of every American who had died or was missing would appear on the memorial; (2) the memorial would make no political statement; (3) no government funds would be used; and (4) the memorial would be in the nation's capital. It would officially be called the Vietnam Veterans Memorial. Once it was finished, however, it became better known as simply the Wall.

It is the condition that the memorial make no political statement that most differentiates it from others. Almost by definition, memorials "celebrate" something, but this one does not. With the exception of the Civil War, the manner in which the Vietnam War divided the country was unprecedented, so it was evident that many, if not most, who were involved did not and do not now celebrate that involvement. By transcending the issue of politics, it was hoped that the Wall would be a means of reconciling the divisions in our country's consciousness. It would be a way of uniting, if such a thing were possible, the divergent thoughts, emotions, and beliefs that emerged during that controversial period.

Moreover, this memorial is completely silent. It is devoid of inspirational quotations or eloquent lines of poetry to tell visitors what it means. An inscription states that the names appear in chronological order by the year of death, and that the memorial was built through private donations of the American people. Other than that, it consists only of the names of those dead and missing. "We were there" is the message it conveys. No interpretation is offered.

In the absence of interpretation, something more is required of those who visit the Wall. They must ask their own questions; they must seek their own answers. This means that whatever your politics, whatever your view of the war, whatever your reason for being at the memorial, you can find something there. The reasons people connect to the gigantic structure are as diverse as the people themselves. It is a way of reconciling the American ambivalence about the war. It is a means of remembering something that for many is almost too painful to be reminded of, realizing still that to forget would be the worst thing of all.

The Wall is a place to which people carry their scars. Veterans arrive daily in wheelchairs and with missing limbs, yet many of the deepest scars are not visible. People visit the Wall in the hope of healing. They go to read the names of those they knew as well as those they will never know. They touch the stone. They etch the names of their loved ones by rubbing the name with a crayon or a pencil onto a piece of paper or a flag.

And people leave things behind. Letters, poems, rings, teddy bears, medals—all these and more are left as messages to the dead. In leaving them, often anonymously and for one person, the one who brought them allows them to be shared again and again by many others.

Part of the miracle of the Wall is its design. Look at it, then close your eyes for a moment. Look again. It won't be the same. It is permanent and, at the same time, constantly changing. Thousands of names are inscribed in smooth black granite that is transformed as the light dims, or a cloud formation passes by. Its appearance is different when hundreds of people are reflected in it than when a solitary figure leans against it.

And rain—it has been said that when it rains, the Wall weeps. The water literally obscures the names. When the rain has stopped and the Wall is still wet, visitors can be seen wiping the water from its surface just to be able to read the names of their loved ones.

Another remarkable aspect of the Wall is its universality, its ability to have an impact on whoever confronts it. In one instance, a father knelt at the Wall beside his daughter. She was too young to understand the conditions of combat, the idea of war, the abrupt and violent end of over 58,000 lives, or the concept of mortality, so he spoke to her of something she *could* understand: daddies. Some of the men whose names appear here, he explained, were daddies, like him. How might she feel if her only relationship to her father was through viewing his name at the Wall? She wept. A connection had been made.

The Wall itself does not attempt to convey any political message, and the same can be said of the following photographs. Not only did the photographer *not* think in terms of heroes, living or dead, he did not think in terms of an ideology of any kind. The images, like the Wall, express no interpretation. They are nonpolitical. They are not intended to convey a singular message.

What Sal Lopes wanted was to create a body of work compelling enough to elicit a response of some kind—sorrow, rage, loss, awe, something. He was not photographing heroes, just people—some with a special connection to the war or to a particular name inscribed on the Wall, others there out of curiosity or to seek a meaning. The purpose of the photographs, if one must be ascribed to them, is much the same as the purpose of the Wall. There is no one message. No appropriate or inappropriate response. Just stop and look at them.

ARLES E SMITH · STANLEY
Z Jr · LEWIS C BARNARD · G
OTER · RAMON DESCHAMPS★ JOSEP
NICE · DONALD · JOHN T KY
DAVID FORTERFIELD · DONALD J PRI
LES R MALBROUGH · HEARNE W BEAVER
NAMAN · DANNIE J BREWINGTON ★JOHN T DOIKES
RANE ★JAMES R CROLEY JESUS DE LA ROSA
LARD ★JACK M BROWN Jr CHARLES
RUHL · DALLAS E GREEN★ BOBBY
SON ★ALLEN L JELINI RAYMOND F J
BARNES MICHAEL J MUMMEL★
N · LEROY E PETERSON · PATRICK T QUINN
BERNARD A GREEN · TURNER L THO
HEN A ZUKOV · JAMES F ASKIN · CLIFFO
S W GEORGE · TIMOTHY S DAVIES · DAVID A D
IFFORD L CARPENTER · BRENT J GRIG
JORGENSEN · BETTY D N

FISH STORY

THOMAS GAVIN

Thomas Gavin was born in Newport News, Virginia, in 1941. Mr. Gavin, who has taught at Middlebury College in Vermont and Delta College in Michigan, is an associate professor of English at the University of Rochester.

Mr. Gavin is the author of the novel *Kingkill*, which was listed among the American Library Association's Notable Books of the Year in 1977 and was also on *Time*'s Editor's Choice list. He has also written *The Last Film of Emile Vico*. His forthcoming novel, *Breathing Water*, will be published by Arcade Books in winter 1994. Mr. Gavin has received fellowships from the Mellon Foundation, the National Endowment for the Arts, and the Bread Loaf Writers Conference. His essay "The Truth Beyond Facts: Journalism and Literature," was listed as a Notable Essay of 1991 in *The Best American Essays 1992* and nominated for a Pushcart Prize. His writing has appeared in *Prairie Schooner*, *Triquarterly*, and the *Georgia Review*.

Mr. Gavin lives in Rochester, New York, with his wife, Susan Holahan. The following selection is an excerpt from his work in progress, *The Bridge of Lost Boys*.

Even though Pardon Wilhelm ran editorials every spring about upstream pollution from the Peterborough Chemical Company that he claimed was giving the waters an ammonia smell and doing god-knew-what to the food chain, there were still people who fished the Genesee River, even people—kids mostly and mostly without their parents' permission—who swam in it. The fishers were old men, grandfathers of the kids who did the swimming, guys who had fished it as boys and refused to believe the world they grew up in was gone. Chub Brotherton was one of them, sixteen years retired from his stock manager job at Homer Winston's hardware store and a lot more of a worry to his wife than he'd been when a steady job kept him approximately sober five days a week and till noon Saturday. He was standing on the morning-shady bank with a bamboo pole, a couple hundred yards down from the War Memorial Bridge, when—so he said—a hand rose out of the water and waved to him.

The hand lurched out of the creamed-coffee stream into a little splash of sunlight that bounced along the surface. It was about ten yards upstream, among the branches of a drowned tree that had lost its grip on the bank and was slipping into the river. It was bruise-colored and puffy, swollen tight against the turned-back shirt cuff. When it dipped back toward the water with an *over-this-way* gesture, it seemed to be asking Chub Brotherton's help to get free of a snag.

Chub Brotherton found himself thinking, he told Pardon later that day, of a clerk he'd known in Winston's Hardware, a man who'd lost a hand in a chainsaw accident, who used to flip the pages of an order form with his stump. It made no sense at all, he knew, to think what he saw in the water was Harlan Slocum's missing hand. But

147

he could never see Harlan Slocum use his stump without thinking of his lost hand, wondering did it get cremated, or buried like a whole body in consecrated ground. "Sometimes," he said with a sly glint, pushing the notion to see if Pardon had any more sense of humor than when he was a kid, "I even used to wonder was it stuck in a back corner of Slocum's deep freeze till the rest of him got ready to join it." When Brotherton saw Pardon laugh, he relaxed a bit and went on, telling how all the time Slocum worked there he never got up nerve to ask. So when Brotherton saw a hand reach out of that muddy water, he couldn't help but think about the body out of sight, the same way he always thought of Slocum's out of sight hand, and he didn't have any great wish to see that body.

Pardon listened to all this patiently, and even—since he could see Chub Brotherton expected it—jotted notes in the spiral reporter's notebook he carried in the side pocket of his sportcoat. He was sitting at Brotherton's dining room table with a glass of iced tea sweating onto a clear, thick, plastic tablecover that protected the intricate lacework of Mrs. Brotherton's tablecloth. She'd been the one who'd produced the iced tea when Pardon declined to join Brotherton in a beer.

"One thing about being retired," Brotherton said. "I can open a beer whenever I want." Pans rasped in the kitchen. "At least," he said, raising his voice and flashing Pardon a we-guys wink, "special days like this I can, when the wife don't object." As soon as Pardon was settled with his iced tea, Mrs. Brotherton had gone back to the kitchen where she could listen without being a part of what was said.

The call from Brotherton had come to Pardon at his desk in the *Rising Sun Times* offices less than an hour earlier, during the slack of time after lunch when it was clear that the day's crises had been handled and there would soon be a paper on the streets. It was just the time of day, maybe the only time of day, when he could spare a few minutes to a fierce old man swearing he'd seen a body in the river, or at least a hand, only he couldn't get anybody to believe it. The way Brotherton's voice huffed and rattled down the phone line, Pardon wasn't sure he believed it either.

"What you should do, Mr. Brotherton," Pardon had said, cradling the phone against his shoulder so he could go on measuring column inches for a wire story he planned to use tomorrow, "is call the police."

"That's who I did call," Brotherton said. "The sheriff department, I mean, not the city police. They're the ones don't believe me." Past Brotherton's liquid wheeze Pardon made out his wife's voice saying, "They're not the only ones."

"Problem is, I'd guess," Pardon said, "the last few days every law officer in the state's manning road blocks. That armored truck business has 'em working double shifts."

The wire story Pardon was working on had been his lead three days running: In the city forty miles north of Rising Sun somebody had pulled off the second-biggest armored truck robbery in history. The empty truck had been left in a cornfield with the two slaughtered guards— one lying by the open cab door, the other twenty yards away as if he'd tried to break for the highway. "Oh," said Brotherton. "That's the story, huh?" Brotherton wasn't one to fill up a telephone wire with words, so while he breathed his ruminative walrus wheeze, Pardon listened to Mrs. Brotherton in the background: "Who'd you expect was gonna believe you when you get like this? You told me you weren't hiding any more bottles—should I believe you?"

Till that moment Pardon had been searching for a way to say thanks and goodbye. Now he hoisted his feet off the open file drawer of his desk and reached for a sheet of copy paper. "Let me get this straight," he said. "You told Sheriff Wakeland about this and he wouldn't even come look?"

"Oh, he sent out a deputy. One of them full-of-hisself kids. We get back to the river, and he decides I'm seeing things without even—"

"Name of Simpkin, this deputy?"

"That's the one," Brotherton said. "Little guy, struts around patting his holster like he's gotta remind hisself where it is."

"I know him," Pardon said. "You still live the corner of Hawthorne and Union?"

"Yeah."

"Give me twenty minutes. I'll be on your porch knocking."

Pardon didn't expect to get a story about a body floating down the Genesee. He did, however, hope that Chub Brotherton had seen something in the river, and that he would be able to find out more about it than Al Wakeland's deputy. Even it didn't turn out to be a crime, it would be a story, and the best part of it would be telling what Sheriff Wakeland's deputy had missed. He wanted to convince Sheriff Wakeland that he couldn't go on letting his deputies turn in reports that were half the time so damn cryptic you couldn't make out what was being reported. The main problem was illiteracy, especially with Deputy Phil Simpkin, but sometimes, Pardon well knew, it was an attempt to cover up just the kind of bouncing-off-the-wall keystone cop stuff that he made it his business to wave under taxpayers' noses.

Since Frank Canby'd gone, Pardon was his own police reporter. It was an exercise in patient diplomacy, calculated betrayals of confidence, and swallowed rage. He made the rounds. By six a.m. every morning he was downtown in Chief Barhite's office shuffling through the overnight reports, taking notes on break-ins and dwi's for the daily crime log. He had an arrangement with Al Barhite that if anything *big* came up, Barhite would give Pardon a call, but two years ago when a couple of guys in ski masks walked into the Kane Bank waving semiautomatics and walked out with thirty-four thousand dollars and change, Barhite had forgot Pardon might want to know. Pardon wouldn't have got the story till he read the next day's reports if Walt Krisp, the ad manager, hadn't come back from lunch complaining he couldn't deposit his paycheck because there'd been a police sawhorse blocking the bank entrance. After collecting his log items from the town police station, Pardon would drive out to the state police post on Route 5 and talk with Sgt. Jake Emmons. Emmons and his men could write a clear report in about two thirds the number of words the town police used. It was a pity the only real news he ever got from them was an occasional single car fatal at the bad turn on Layhill Road. From the state police post Pardon swung back toward town. He saved his stop at the county jail for last because two or three times a week neither he nor Sheriff Wakeland could make out one of the deputy reports was describing, and Pardon would have to give it up or wait till the deputy, usually Phil Simpkin, got in from a run to translate.

On his way over to Chub Brotherton's house Pardon stopped off at the jail. He knocked on the countertop and sang out, "Anybody home? Everybody out on the barricades?" and asked Madge Purvis to show him the reports. She was the mother of Deputy Graham Purvis and extended her motherly protection to the entire department. She liked blouses with florid bows knotted at the neck and had arms like fleshy water balloons that ended in delicate, tapering fingers with tapering nails that slowed her typing. She gave them a pink gloss. She looked up from her typewriter over the tops of her half-glasses. "So he's back," she said. "You spell somebody's name wrong? 'Cause I gotta tell you, the overnight stuff is already—"

"No problem, Madge," said Pardon with a smile he hoped was fuddled and innocent. "I just want to see the stuff you got so far today. Working out a new schedule, maybe."

"I don't know," Madge said. Under the edge of her desk her empty shoes lay still as a pair of sleeping guard dogs. Next to them her stockinged feet were crossed and resting on their outer ankles so Pardon could see the ruddy ball of a toe.

"Just want to check how much stuff comes in before two p.m. Maybe work out some way to keep from pestering you folks before you've had your morning coffee."

Madge looked over her shoulder to the sheriff's closed door. "You talk to Sheriff Wakeland about this?"

"Well, not yet, Madge. No point in bothering him if it's not going to work out. This is just a survey, just to see how much work we get by mid-afternoon."

Pardon saw Madge's feet grope for her shoes. She brought him the wire basket of reports as if she were carrying a tray of hors d'oeuvres too prettily arranged to disturb, and set herself to watch what he did with them.

Pardon scanned the reports, pausing at one or two that didn't interest him so the one that did wouldn't seem special. Halfway through the stack he found it, logged at 10:37. It read: "Herman Brotherton, 47 Hawthorne, fishing below War Mem. bridge saw hand in water. Went with him to spot Could mot find spot he saw. Sunk kimb must be it. Subject was maybe dinking but not disorder. Took subjet back home."

"Here's another funny one," Pardon chuckled. "Looks like old Chub Brotherton's been telling fish stories. What happened, he just want some company strolling the river path?"

Madge remained unamused. "You'll have to ask Deputy Simpkin," she said.

"Not worth it," Pardon said, lifting the report as if he were about to move on to the next. "Sounds like the only story there is Old Chub's cracking the bottle before noon these days."

"You can say that again," Madge said. "He calls here, it took him five minutes to get straight it's not just a hand floating on the water, it's somebody drowned, he thinks. You know, I try and discourage the wild goose chaser calls, but sometimes it just ain't possible."

"He think a floating body was going to stay in one place while he went for the sheriff?"

"Listen," Madge said. "One thing I know dealing with these guys. When they're seeing pink elephants, it's no good asking how they got there or where they're going."

Pardon smiled and chuckled. "Now what do you suppose," he said, "Phil means by this 'sunk kimb'?"

Madge plucked the report out of Pardon's hand, studied it impatiently, then said: "That's *limb*. Sunk limb. Some tree limb. The guy claimed the body was caught in some tree limb or something." She pushed the report back at Pardon as if she'd just translated a bit of technical jargon for a novice. "Lord knows," she said, "Phil's got more to do than fiddle over his typing. You got any idea how many hours those boys spent on roadblocks the past two days? My Graham, he spent the night at the Layhill–County Line Road intersection? He was back on the job this morning after three and a half hours sleep."

"Yeah?" Pardon said. "Any idea how much longer the sheriff's gonna keep it up?"

"He says maybe today's the last day. They musta slipped through, he says. And I'll be glad when it's over, 'cause I ain't sleeping much either. Every time they stop a car, it could be the one that comes out shooting. So you think we got time for wild goose rhymes out here, you think again."

Pardon blinked, thought again, and asked Madge to tell him what convinced Deputy Simpkin the old guy hadn't seen a body, thinking if he had any sense he'd forget Chub Brotherton and do a roadblock interview, and maybe he could swing out Layhill Road on the way back, and why in hell couldn't Frank Canby have hung on another month?

"Phil, too," Madge was saying. "None of the boys is sleeping right. He was with Graham last night, and you should see the circles. Circles under the eyes, both of them. But he's gotta drive all the way out to the river, and the old guy's not sure if it's this tree or that one the body's caught in. He finally says here's the spot and all Phil can see is a piece of driftwood about two inches underwater. 'There's your hand,' he tells him. 'Don't that look just like a hand, that sunken log?' And the old guy says, 'Maybe this is the wrong spot.' Well, Phil's no dummy. You can play that game all day."

"Sure," Pardon said. "I can just see Phil Simpkin tramping up and down that bank all day looking for a floater. How far they get anyhow, before Phil called off the search?"

Madge paused a second, then said, "You'll have to ask Deputy Simpkin." After another pause she said, "You about done here? Phil's not the only one got work to do today, you know."

Pardon thumbed through the remaining reports, thanked Madge, and drove two blocks past his own house on Hawthorne Street to the corner lot where Chub Brotherton had lived since Pardon was in grade school. One of the reasons Pardon was making a special visit to Chub's house was because he'd owed Chub a couple of favors for the last forty-five years or so.

When Pardon was ten, an eighth grader named Butch Carson showed him the path across the corner lot that was the big kids' shortcut to Hamilton School. The story was that Old Man Brotherton shied stones from his driveway at kids who used it. That made the shortcut hard to pass up. Soon as it was bike weather in the spring, you'd zip through the hole in the bushes and pedal fast as lightning. A dip in the path left you one breathless moment pedaling in air, and you hit ground with just enough control to brake and duck through the other line of bushes. One

Saturday after a rain Pardon came off the dip tromping his brake in a puddle and skidded into a tangle of branches. He was stunned and scraped in a dozen places and had a foot caught in his bike chain when behind him Old Man Brotherton's storm door banged. He held back tears and lay still. The man looming above him parted the bushes. The first words Pardon ever heard Chub Brotherton say he still remembered. "Well, son," he said, "you got the speediest wheels on the block. But you oughta learn one thing today: When you don't know what kind of muck you're coming down in, don't come down fast."

After he untangled Pardon's foot from the bike chain, he took him inside and washed his cuts at the kitchen sink, asking Pardon questions he answered for himself in a gruff gentle voice. "That sting?" he'd say, and then, "You bet it does." Then with another jab of iodine-soaked cotton, "Feeling pretty sorry for yourself?" And then: "Yup." And after a second: "Gonna give up riding that bike like hell on wheels? Nope." When he was done, he called to Mrs. Brotherton, who at the first sight of blood had gasped and brought the iodine, but applied it in such timid daubs that Brotherton had taken over the job: "Marilyn, let's see if this guy can eat as many of your oatmeal cookies as I can." In Pardon's house grownups always stopped at two. Not Mister Brotherton.

Then years later, a senior in high school, one January night Pardon was hitching home from a bar in Geneseo and Chub Brotherton stopped for him. "You're the Wilhelm kid, ain'tcha?" he said, and then, as before, answered his own question: "So, hiya, Wilhelm kid. You look drunker'n I am. Are you? You damn bet." On the drive home they talked about the high school football team and Pardon didn't even have to ask Mr. Brotherton to drop him off a few houses past his own so his folks wouldn't hear a car door slam. He'd said goodnight and was just stepping out of the car when Chub Brotherton said the second thing that Pardon, considering it now, counted as part of what he owed him, even though he'd never been smart enough to profit from the advice: "You know, Wilhelm kid," he said. "You got a good head. But you're still skidding into muck fast as you can go. You're way too young to be drinking like all your future's in your past, you know? But you keep on like this, that's where it'll be." And Pardon, thinking himself a man in a man-to-man talk, had tossed back a grin and said, "Don't do as I do, do as I say, huh, Mister B.? Thanks for the lift," and shut the car door.

That was the last time Pardon spoke to Chub Brotherton until today. In the years since he'd returned to Rising Sun, he saw Brotherton now and then in his backyard, wandering among his tomato plants and pole beans as if he'd lost something there. A couple of times Pardon waved as he drove past, but Brotherton always cocked his head with a puzzled squint, and Pardon guessed maybe his eyes weren't good on distances anymore. If he remembered the two conversations he'd had with Chub Brotherton, it wasn't because they meant much to him at the time. But in the years his marriage was coming apart, more than once Pardon found that what Brotherton said turned out to explain Pardon to himself better than any words of his own. He'd wake up hung over with a flat wallet, and say to himself, "I'm still skidding into muck." It took having the experience to make sense of the words, but having the words, at last, made sense of the experience. Knowing that living in the big city he would never find the discipline to keep from skidding into deeper and deeper muck was one of the things that had brought Pardon back to Rising Sun. He'd never thought of Chub Brotherton as having much part in that decision, but today when he recognized the old man's voice on the phone, he realized with some surprise that he owed him a favor. If these days when Pardon waved hello Brotherton was looking past him or through him, back when Pardon was a kid Brotherton looked *at* him, and saw clearly enough where he was headed, and took the trouble, with little enough thanks from Pardon, to try to head him off.

So Pardon clumped up the front porch steps of the old corner house and rang the bell.

It was Chub Brotherton's wife who came to the door. The hair he remembered as streaked gray was now stark white, held in a wispy, balding flip she might have got from a World War II fashion spread in *Life*. She was a tall woman hunched inside a cotton housedress dappled with pink and yellow flowers. She gave him such a blinking, dream-shadowed look he thought he must have waked her from a nap. He caught himself almost whispering his name, but before he finished she pulled open the door and said, "He's back in the dining room," and without the screen door veiling her face Pardon saw it had been recent tears making her blink.

Pardon looked past her down a narrow living room much the same as he remembered it. Furniture crowded the room as if it were a loosely packed moving van: a bloated sofa covered with a piece of clear plastic, armchairs sprawled like fat men who couldn't close their legs, an upright piano squeezed against the far wall. The huge fireplace had white painted bricks and a capped gas pipe sticking out of the hearth. A couple dozen color photos cluttered the mantel—high school graduation mug shots, kids in ascending sizes sardined along a picnic table with mom in the middle, and dad only a pinhead shadow stretched toward them across the grass. On top of the piano were two black and white pictures—one of a young man with a couple pounds of high-gloss hair and Presley sideburns, the other of the same young man, shorn and leaner, harder around the mouth, in military uniform. Pardon remembered from when he'd been there as a kid the black and white photos and the smell he used to think of as old-people smell because it was in his grandparents' house, too. Now he recognized it as mildew.

"Come on in, pull up a stool," Chub Brotherton called, and Pardon made his way around a vinyl hassock and an armchair to the dining room archway. Chub Brotherton was sitting at the head of the dinner table with a can of beer and a glass. A portable television set on the sideboard was tuned to a sports channel with the sound a murmur. Brotherton was older, too—his dark eyes sucked deep under the brow ridge, the cords of his neck slack. Pardon thought of an ancient turtle. "You still drink beer, don'tcha? Marilyn, how about pouring the Wilhelm kid a beer."

Pardon took the chair at Brotherton's right hand, his back to the kitchen door. He negotiated his way out of a beer and accepted a glass of iced tea, and noted that Mrs. Brotherton had kept her habit of leaving her husband alone with his guests, as if she were either terribly busy or didn't quite approve of them. Brotherton said, "You're looking more like your dad these days than *he* looked, last time I saw him. How many years has it been since they moved to Florida, your folks?"

"Fifteen, I guess," Pardon said. "They left the same year I came back home to run the paper. I been living in the old house ever since."

Brotherton shook his head. "Never could figure why people'd leave the place they spent their whole lives in to go die under a palm tree."

"They got to like it down there, visiting my grandma," Pardon said. "Then when my grandma died, my mom inherited her house. You know how it is—they couldn't afford to keep 'em both, and I was willing to take this one."

Brotherton nodded as if he were hearing of a misfortune. Then he told Pardon his story of the hand waving in the water and how he thought it might belong to Harlan

Slocum. When he was done, he took another sip of beer and said, "So: you gonna be like that deputy? You think I was too drunk out there to see what I said I seen?"

"I don't know," Pardon said. "You seem steady enough now. Were you?"

Brotherton grinned and took a sip of beer. "I remember you," he said. "Still a smartmouth, huh? Well, that's okay. You were a *smart* smartmouth. And you got a right to ask." He leaned toward Pardon, the turtle eyes peering across the table from deep inside his skull. "Well, I wasn't drunk. Right now I'm a *little* the other side of cold sober, but this morning I was dry as a stone in the sun. I got in my fishing gear this little pint bottle of Four Roses, see? And when I go fishin', I take just one swallow when I start down that path, the one down from the parking lot to the bridge. I don't take it to get drunk, I like to *fish*, not booze. But a little swallow helps me get down that path to the water. That little swallow's *all* I had under my belt when I saw that hand wave at me. You believe that?"

"Yes," Pardon said.

"Well, after I saw — what I saw — I had to hike back up that hill to my car, and I drove over to Joe's filling station to call the sheriff. Then I went back to the parking lot by the bridge and took one more swallow while I waited for that deputy to meet me there. I was rattled, and I'd climbed that hill a damn sight faster'n I usually do, and I knew I was gonna have to go down it again. But that second swallow was my mistake. That damn deputy smelled it on me, and he wouldn't believe a thing I said. You hear what I'm saying?"

"Yes," Pardon said. "But Simpkin said you had trouble finding the spot. If you were cold sober, wouldn't — "

"You been *talking* to him ain't you?" Brotherton said. It made Pardon feel he'd betrayed a confidence. "You been talkin' to that s.o.b."

"I stopped in and read his report, that's all," Pardon confessed. "Couldn't make head or tail what he was saying."

"That don't surprise me," Brotherton said. "That boy was stiff as a wire brush from the start. He gets out of the car all official, wants to lead *me* to the body. I said the body was near the bridge, so he decides it's right *under* the bridge, thinks it's somebody jumped *off* the bridge. So he heads down the wrong path—the steep one, y'know? The one leads straight down to the water. Well I'm no kid anymore, I'm eighty-three years young next month. I went after him down that steep path, and I made it to the bottom, which is more'n most guys my age could do. But this damn deputy's already looked all up and down the bank on both sides of the bridge, and he says, 'Ain't no body down here, Pop.' Here I am, trying to catch my breath, and when I finally get out that we gotta walk downstream a ways, he gets real mean. 'Ohhh,' he says. 'Now it's down this way, huh? You really sure you saw anything at all, Pop? Or you been hitting the sauce?' Well, that's when I got mad."

"So what happened," Pardon said, "when you got to the place where you'd seen the body? It was just gone?"

"That's what I'm trying to tell you," Brotherton said. "We never *got* there."

"What?"

"We hiked a little ways along the river, and the deputy's saying, 'Nobody coulda jumped *this* far,' and I'm saying, 'I'm not telling you anybody jumped anywhere, I just know I seen a body and it's caught in one of the trees that's dropped over the water.' So he points downstream, down to that first bend, and there's another tree out over the water there, and he says, 'You mean like that one?' and I say, 'Yeah.' *Like* that one, I meant, but he gets up to the bend and he looks in the water all around the tree and he says, 'Look, Pop, you can see for yourself, there ain't no body here, and I'm a busy man.' And that was it."

"You mean he wouldn't go any further?"

Brotherton nodded. He swallowed hard, like he was

swallowing down something that wanted to come back on him. "First he shows me a damn underwater tree branch and says that's what I seen. Then he took me by the arm," Brotherton said. "He turned me around and marched me. Felt like a punk kid getting marched to the principal's office." Brotherton's voice was husky and shaking. His eyes deep in their holes were bright. "I kept telling him we had to go thirty yards further down. All he'd say was, 'I'm s'posed to be watching out for these armored car robbers, I got no time for patty-cake games, Pop.' I couldn't tell him a thing."

"Easy," Pardon said.

Chub Brotherton breathed hard. "I ain't drunk," he said fiercely. "That deputy marched me up on the porch and rang the bell of my own house before I could get out my key. The wife opens the door, and first thing he says is, 'You'll have to keep an eye on him a while, lady. He's pretty tanked up.' So the wife, she thinks I broke my promise to her. I said I'd never have to get brought home by a cop again, and I ain't been on a flat, blackout drunk in eight years. Can't tell *her* nothin' either. So I figured if I was gonna have to take all the crying and fussing, I might as well get the fun, and I opened a beer. Halfway through it I called you. This is only my second." He took a swallow, a small one. Pardon could see there was no sweat on the glass. It would be half warm by now. "You believe me?" Brotherton asked.

Pardon said: "What do you say we go back to the river and look around?"

On the far side of the Great War Memorial Bridge was a stone-paved parking lot and a clearing just big enough for a picnic bench and a trash barrel. Pardon left his car in the lot and followed Chub Brotherton down the sloping path to the river bank. Brotherton walked a bit stiff, turning sideways to step-slide in the steep places, but sure of himself, knowing without hesitation where he could plant each step, holding the branches that would snap back in Pardon's face until he could raise an arm against them. He was a big man, even in his shrunken age thick across the shoulders, and along the level stretches of the path he swung his arms when he walked and went light-footed, almost on the balls of his feet, in a wrestler's strut that made Pardon think that from behind he might be mistaken for a much younger man.

The way his lips had tightened when Pardon offered to come back to the river with him was almost too grim for a smile. Pardon couldn't tell if he was grateful, or terrified that he'd been proved a fool. He'd picked up his glass as if he meant to drain the last of his beer, then put it down and said, "Before we go I gotta hit the can for a minute."

Sitting alone at the dining room table, Pardon listened for Mrs. Brotherton behind him in the kitchen. For a while during his conversations with Chub Brotherton she'd been doing dishes, hissing water in the drain and rapping pans in a way that made his talk with her husband almost confidential. Pardon hadn't noticed when the last clatter of silver in the strainer gave way to the listening silence. With Chub Brotherton upstairs in the bathroom and him alone at the table, the silence in the other room made Pardon squirm. The television murmur calling strokes in a dull golf match didn't help. He wondered if his not going in to pass the time of day was rude. He wondered if her not coming out was rude, or if she were just too absorbed in something to remember he was there. There was a cough, a rattle of paper. Pardon got up, presented himself at the kitchen doorway with a smile. Mrs. Brotherton was sitting at the kitchen table, a cup of coffee by her wrist. She was peering down her bifocals at the pages of the *Rising Sun Times* as if she didn't see much there she liked. Pardon turned his greeting into a deferential grunt, nodded, and veered off into the living room.

He was standing at the piano, staring into the eyes of the young man in his crisp Marine uniform and wondering why he looked back at the photographer with such a cold impatience to get on with it so the young man could run out and join whatever moment of history was waiting for him beyond the photographer's lens. Judging by the age of the photo, he figured the history the young man had run to join must have been Vietnam and wondered if that explained why the rest of the piano top wasn't strewn with shots of him with a wife and children. He felt Mrs. Brotherton at his elbow.

"There's no point to it," she said. Her voice was husky, hardly above a whisper, and her eyes flicked to the stairway her husband would be coming down. "He's already had too hard a day, a man his age. You'd be doing him a kindness just to let him stay home and get his afternoon nap."

Pardon wondered how a woman could live with a man more than fifty years and not know this was more important to Chub Brotherton than his afternoon nap. He wondered if he dared say that to a woman old enough to be his mother.

"I can't stop him going out there, Mrs. Brotherton," he said, "and I promised to go with him. When we're done I'll see that he's — "

"It's going to waste your time anyway," she said, and her hands, clenched under her breast, sprang apart as if she were ripping a crooked seam. "He didn't see him this time any more than the others."

"There been other times?"

"He's always talking at him," she said. She jerked her head at the photo on the piano. "I'd come downstairs in the morning. Hearing him on the stairs, you'd think he'd come home and they was already in a big argument. Like that last summer before he joined up. Always after him to get a real job, get some ambition. I used to tell him he drove Johnny out of the house." She lowered her eyes, her lip twitching. "Then I walk in the door and he's all alone — just clearing out his throat, he says to me one time."

"Are you telling me," Pardon said, "this isn't the first time Mister Brotherton thought he was seeing — "

"It's got worse this past year. Last April he was out back digging. At first I thought he was just spading the garden. When it kept getting deeper, I went out. He was talking to him, like always, just like he was there. 'What's all this?' I said. 'You don't need it that deep for tomatoes.' He turns around, his eyes red with crying. 'He's on his way home, Marilyn,' he says. 'This time I know it. We gotta have a place ready — place for Johnny to rest.'"

Upstairs a toilet flushed, a door opened.

"That's how it is when it's an MIA," she said in a quick whisper. "It's never over. He never comes home, he never dies. Sometimes you wish and wish he'd just be dead so you can get some sleep. That old man don't need another walk in the woods, Mister Wilhelm. He needs some sleep."

"All right, Wilhelm's kid," Chub Brotherton sang out, and Pardon turned around to see him almost trip off the last stair, flattening the zipper on his fly. "Let's go for a hike."

When they got level with the river the path was wide enough for them to walk side by side. It had been a warm morning, but in the last hour the sun had gone and come and gone again, racing from one clear patch in the sky to another, and it was cool under the trees.

"It's a little ways yet," Brotherton said. Then, after they'd walked in silence a couple minutes, he said: "You'd be — what? — about seven, eight years younger'n my boy?"

"I guess," Pardon said. "I remember, now you mention it, a Brotherton in eighth grade about the time I must have been in first or second. Never guessed he was living two blocks down from me. On the football team, was he?"

"That's right. In high school, too. Left end was his position. Homecoming game his senior year, he caught the winning pass, you remember? 21-20, the score was."

"Guess I was too young," Pardon said. "When you're a little kid, the big kids, they live in a different universe. Your boy was one of the big kids."

Brotherton chuckled without much mirth. "Thought he was, anyhow. I could never tell him a damn thing." Sudden light shook down through the trees. Sun dappled the path and leaves. Then clouds rushed to block it out. "He enlisted back in '52, I thought, Good—coupla years in the service, it'll make a man out of him. Never figured he'd go right back in once his time was up. Twenty years and out, that was his plan. He had it figured he could retire a couple years before I did. He had everything figured, till Vietnam."

Pardon swallowed. The pollution smell from the river seemed to coat the back of his throat. He notched his memory to pry up a fresh angle on the Peterborough Chemical Plant, get a story out of it or at least another editorial.

"Twenty years and out, that how he saw it," Chub Brotherton was saying. "Only thing in his life he ever stuck with, aside from football. That marriage of his, we just got a postcard. Not even in church, you know? Just say some words in front of a judge too dumb to be a lawyer. No wonder it didn't last the year."

"Where was he posted then?"

"Carolina for a while. Fort-something-or-other. It'll come to me. You know I got a grandson old enough to vote, that I ain't never seen?"

Brotherton stopped, reached a hand to Pardon's arm. He was looking straight ahead.

"There it is," he said, and his grip on Pardon's arm tightened. "Up by that next bend. See that tree limb dropped in the water? That's where I seen him."

Trees grew out of the brush and weeds on both sides of the path, willow and oak and cottonwood. About twenty yards ahead, where the bank curved, an ancient willow seemed to have slid off the edge of the path. The trunk, so big it would have taken three or four men to circle it with their arms, angled about thirty degrees over the water.

Brotherton let go of Pardon's arm and walked ahead. He walked stiffly, suspending each footfall. Pardon after a few moments followed. He had an odd feeling that he was bringing up the end of a solemn procession. Brotherton stopped at the trunk of the willow.

A thick limb, split chest-high from the trunk, lay in the water. Brotherton groped a hand to it, steadying himself at the place where the wood had wrenched and twisted like petrified taffy out of the bark, and raddled with worm tracks and woodpecker rings.

"Right out there," Brotherton said. His voice under the arching limbs had a tense reverence. Pardon looked in the direction he was staring, but saw in the stream only a shadowy tangle of dead branches. Shadows under the tree made the water silver-black. Fresh shoots, he noticed, grew from the dead limb right up to the place where it dropped into the water. A larger limb, high overhead, curved down from the trunk and dipped its branches like splayed fingers in the current. Here too Pardon noticed that while green shoots still sprang from the upper branches, those that touched the water were leafless sticks, as if they had bathed in a river of acid. He tried to imagine a dead hand reaching up to clasp the dead branches.

"I don't see anything," Pardon said, but as he spoke reflected light winked along the undersides of the leaves, and all over the opaque surface of the stream sunlight opened jigsaw holes. The sand below was ribbed with a frozen echo of the ripples bouncing against the bank. Strands of moss danced on a sunken branch. At a wavering edge of the hole of sunlight he looked through Pardon saw that the ripples had been erased by a wide groove plowed in the sand. He looked up along that groove, out about twenty feet, and saw what might be a wrist, a wrist the same gray as a branch, the shirtsleeve hooked in it, the wrist and the branch bobbing together in the current, the hand groping downward, fingertips almost touching the water.

"Sweet Christ," Pardon whispered. He was, he'd learned long ago, a man who thought quicker and better sitting behind a desk than on his feet. So when Chub Brotherton gave a strange, lowing moan that broke on a sob and strode down the bank into the water, wallowing out to where the hand hung, Pardon stood on the path watching. He waited, frozen, while Brotherton reached both arms into the water, tried to lift something and lost his grip, then crouched, ducked forward, head in the water, and came up coughing, holding what he'd found in a tight hug, its arm over one of his shoulders, its cheek resting almost tenderly, like a sleeping baby, on the other, and water streaming off them both. Pardon wanted not to look at the face, but made himself. That was once a man, he told himself. He had brown hair, a ragged beard. It was only when he saw Brotherton try to turn, and lurch almost to his knees, that Pardon broke from his trance and splashed into the water after him.

At first Brotherton didn't seem to understand that Pardon was trying to help. When Pardon grabbed the body under the armpits to take it from him, Brotherton twisted away, bellowing, and almost slipped from the shallows into the deep cut of the stream. Pardon grabbed tight, held on till Brotherton steadied himself, then felt the old man gradually relax his hold on his burden so Pardon could share it. Together they half carried, half dragged the body to shore and laid it on its back on the path, and sprawled themselves on either side of it.

A huge flat rock was lashed across the body's chest and

167

belly. Pardon ran his fingers over the frayed clothesline that held it, touched the rock, marveling at when it could have appeared there. It took a moment to realize he'd seen it before, while they were struggling toward the bank, and even cursed it for making the body so heavy. But he was already remembering the shock of that immersion and the staggering journey to the bank as something that happened long ago to a person he barely recognized as himself. He and Brotherton were panting, shivering with clamped jaws from the chill, late-September stream, while the body between them lay in a still, dreaming calm. They looked at each other across it, both dripping, blinking water from their eyelashes, trying to recognize in each other's face something of the relationship they'd had before and seeing only strangeness, as if their common immersion in the acid-laced river had been a baptism that changed you forever. Pardon wondered if his own face had the same haunted pallor. The sun was gone again, they were in a world gone gray. Brotherton carefully let himself down from his elbow and stretched out. This time his moan became not a sob but a long shivering sigh. He's a man in his eighties, Pardon thought. He never got his afternoon nap.

Pardon controlled his chattering teeth and said, "I'll take you home. We'll call the cops. From there. Then get warm."

Brotherton jerked himself back onto his elbow and said, "No." His voice was a harsh commanding croak. "You go. Bring back that—Bring with you," he said, his chest heaving. He gulped air, breathed deep a couple times, then started again, calmer, with a clamped rage. "I'm not leaving this guy's side," he said. His hand was heavy on the body's shoulder. "He's not getting out of my sight. Not till you get back here. With that. That damn deputy."

Pardon, despite Chub Brotherton's fierce glare, felt howls of laughter bubbling up from his gut. He stifled them, got to his feet.

"Listen to me," he said. He was trying to find words other than the ones Mrs. Brotherton would use to tell Chub Brotherton that he was an old man who'd worn himself out tramping up and down steep paths and had just got a dunking in water so cold he might any minute go into shock. "Listen," he said. "I gotta take you back with me. I don't want to come back here and find—"

"No," Chub Brotherton said. "You listen for once. You always were a good boy, Wilhelm's kid. But you never listened to me either. Now do what I say."

"Yes," Pardon said. "The deputy. I'll do my best."

Chub Brotherton nodded, still holding Pardon's eyes. "I shoulda gone in for him the first time," he said. Something more than the chill was making him shiver. It struggled to get past Brotherton's clenched jaws. "I tried," he croaked. "Couldn't make myself. I thought—" and his eyes winced with grief. He shook it off. "I was scared," he said. "Scared it might be somebody I knew."

Pardon made himself look at the body, the flat stone pressing it to the earth. He made himself look at the face: a young man, his jaw dropped in astonishment; death the last thing he could have imagined. A young man. Pardon looked at Brotherton's hand on the young man's shoulder. He raised an arm—a murky promise to return that paused, hung a moment on the air in something like a salute—and started up the path, walking at first, walking fast, then breaking into a heavy trot, his wet trousers clinging to his legs, rasping at each stride, leaving the old man to guard a stranger's son as if he were his own.

Glossary

abstemious — moderate, especially in eating and drinking

aesthetic — sensitive to art and beauty; showing good taste

ambivalence — simultaneous conflicting feelings toward a person or thing

archipelago — a group or chain of many islands

ascribe — assign or attribute

austere — having a severe or stern look or manner

blasé — satiated and bored

boistrous — noisy and unruly; rowdy

bulwark — a person or thing serving as a strong defense or protection

cataclysm — any violent upheaval

chauvinism — prejudiced devotion to any attitude or cause

détente — a lessening of tension or hostility between nations as through treaties or trade agreements

efface — to wipe out, obliterate

effrontery — unashamed boldness, audacity

fecund — fruitful or fertile

fortitude — the strength to bear misfortune calmly and patiently; firm courage

gainsay — contradict or oppose

garrison — a fortified place with troops and guns

gauche — lacking social grace, awkward, tactless

gulag — the Soviet penal system under Stalin; a network of prisons and forced labor camps

indomitable — not easily discouraged, defeated or subdued

intrinsic — not dependent on external circumstances; essential, inherent

joie de vivre — joy of living

Ka'bah — the sacred Moslem shrine at Mecca, toward which believers turn when praying

lucid — readily understood; clear

maverick — a person who takes an independent stand, as in politics

Mecca—one of the two capitals of Saudi Arabia, near the Red Sea; birthplace of Mohammed and hence a holy city of Islam

minimalism—a movement in art, dance, music, and literature beginning in the 1960s in which only the simplest design and forms are used

monochromatic—of or having one color

mosque—a Muslim temple or place of worship

muezzin—in Muslim countries, a crier who calls the people to prayer five times a day

oblique—not straight to the point; indirect

opulent—characterized by abundance or profusion; luxurient

ostentation—showy display of wealth or knowledge

parquet—a floor of inlaid design

perfidious—treacherous, breaking of faith

pillage—deprive of money or property by violence; loot

pious—having or showing religious devotion

propagate—to spread ideas or customs from one place to another

reticent—having a restrained, quiet, or understated quality

scion—a descendant, offspring

straiten—to bring into difficulties, cause to be in distress or want

sublime—noble, exalted, majestic

sybarite—anyone very fond of self-indulgence and luxury

transcend—go beyond the limits of

translucent—transparent, shining through

untenable—cannot be held, defended, or maintained

vanquish—to conquer or defeat

zealot—fanatic; ardently devoted to a purpose

zenith—the highest point

Further Reading

Insofar as the pantheon of heroes is large and a comprehensive list of books about them is more than could be accommodated in the space of a few pages, we have instead concentrated on books for further reading about heroes and heroism and other topics by the authors included in this volume of Icarus.

Bach, Steven. *Marlene Dietrich: Life and Legend.* New York: William Morrow & Co., 1992. Nonfiction: In interviews from around the world and with Ms. Dietrich herself, the author focuses on the woman and the myth.

—. *Final Cut: Dreams and Disaster in the Making of Heavens Gate.* New York: E.P. Dutton, 1987. Relates film-making events from May 1977, when the author was appointed vice president of East Coast and European production for United Artists, to when he was named head of worldwide production.

Burton, Richard, ed. *The Arabian Nights.* Provo, UT: Regal Publications, 1992. Fiction: The classic retelling of the collection of stories told by Scheherazade for one thousand and one consecutive nights.

—. *Personal Narrative of a Pilgrimage to Al-Madinah and Meccah.* New York: Dover Publishing. Nonfiction: The preeminent Victorian Orientalist, fluent in Arabic, disguises himself in 1853 to become the first Englishman to visit the sacred cities of Mecca and Medina.

Campbell, Joseph. *The Hero with a Thousand Faces.* Princeton, NJ: Princeton University Press, 1973. Nonfiction: An examination through ancient hero myths of the eternal human struggle for identity.

Carlyle, Thomas. *On Heroes, Hero Worship, and the Heroic in History.* Lincoln: University of Nebraska Press, 1966. Nonfiction: A collection of lectures that help readers to understand both the faults and the virtues of the times.

Constantine, Peter. *Japanese Street Slang.* New York: Weatherhill Inc., 1992. Nonfiction: The first exposé of raw street-language as it is used in Japan today.

Hamilton, Edith. *Mythology.* New York: E.P. Dutton, 1989.

Nonfiction: A collection of the mythical tales of the gods, heroes, and mortals of ancient Greece.

Hendricks, Rhoda A. *Classical Gods and Heroes: Myths as Told by the Ancient Authors.* New York: Frederick Ungar Publishing Co, 1972. Nonfiction: Told in the words and style of the ancient authors, the classical myths enable the reader to recapture the wonder that the heroic adventures and misadventures inspired in the original authors.

Levy, Emanuel. *John Wayne: Prophet of the American Way of Life.* Metuchen, NJ: Scarecrow Press Inc., 1988. Nonfiction: An examination of John Wayne's impact on American culture.

Lopes, Sal. *The Wall: Images and Offerings from the Vietnam Veterans Memorial.* New York: Collins Publishers, Inc., 1987. Nonfiction: Photographs of visitors to the memorial with excerpts from the messages they leave behind.

McGhee, Richard. *John Wayne: Actor, Artist, Hero.* London: McFarland & Co. Publishers, 1990. Nonfiction: An indepth consideration of John Wayne as man and myth.

Owens, Louis. *Other Destinies: Understanding the American Indian Novel.* Norman: University of Oklahoma Press, 1992. Nonfiction: A critical analysis of novels written by American Indians between 1854 and today.

—. *The Sharpest Sight.* Norman: University of Oklahoma Press, 1992. Fiction: Through solving the mystery of a murder, the characters learn who they are as mixed-bloods in contemporary America.

Prange, Gordon. *At Dawn We Slept: The Untold Story of Pearl Harbor.* New York: Viking Penguin, 1991. Nonfiction: An authoritative record of how Japan planned and executed the infamous attack on Pearl Harbor.

—. *Miracle at Midway.* New York: Penguin Books, 1982. Nonfiction: The author brings together eyewitness accounts from the men who commanded and the men who fought on both sides.

Scammell, Michael. *Solzhenitsyn: A Biography.* New York: W.W. Norton & Co., 1986. Nonfiction: The life of Aleksandr Solzhenitsyn based on information made available to the author by Solzhenitsyn and his family.

Solzhenitsyn, Aleksandr. *The Gulag Archipelago.* New York: HarperCollins, 1991. The author recounts his own prison experiences and those of 227 other survivors of the gulag in three volumes from 1945 to 1953.

—. *One Day in the Life of Ivan Denisovich.* New York: Farrar Straus & Giroux, 1991. Fiction: A picture of life in a Soviet work camp and a moving tribute to a man's will to prevail over relentless dehumanization.

Wolfe, Tom. *The Bonfire of the Vanities.* New York: Farrar Straus & Giroux, 1987. Fiction: A young investment banker is involved in a freak accident and caught in the comedic whirlwind of the press, politicians, police, clergy, and assorted hustlers of New York City.

—.*The Electric Kool-Aid Acid Test.* New York: Bantam Books, 1983. Nonfiction: The seminal work on American hippie culture.

—.*The Painted Word.* New York: Bantam Books, 1982. Nonfiction: The author charts the erratic course of the social history of modern art from the beginning of its revolution against literary content in art to its present state in which it has become a parody of itself.

—. *Radical Chic and Mau-Mauing the Flak Catchers.* New York: Farrar Straus & Giroux, 1987. Nonfiction: Two extensive essays related in theme and substance provide a historical perspective on the impulse of the upper classes to identify themselves with what they imagine to be the raw vital life-style of the lower class and highlight the radical and ethnic game-playing in America's new class wars.

—. *The Right Stuff.* New York: Farrar Straus & Giroux, 1983. Nonfiction: The full story of the first Americans in space.

175

Index